Rain Comes to Yamboorah

Rain Comes to Yamboorah

Reginald Ottley

Illustrated by Robert Hales

Harcourt, Brace & World, Inc., New York

To a man I'll always remember

Contents

Chapter One

"Two Livin', Shinin' Beauts"

The boy smiled. He had neat white teeth set in a brown, freckled face. Under the thatch of his fair tousled hair, his eyes held a kind of faraway remoteness, as if he were seeing beyond the crows perched on the killing pens to a dream of his own, hazed with the mirages floating in the sky.

"Yeah," he said down to Rags. "I reckon I could. With a bit of luck, I c'n ride him in time for the muster."

He was thinking and talking about a roan colt the boss had given him some weeks before. The colt had a deformed hoof: the frog, or spongy center of the sole, was overgrown. Under Kanga's skillful care, the hoof was now almost healed.

Excited by the thought of at last riding the colt, the boy began again to chop wood. Regularly his ax rose and fell in steady rhythm, and Rags shifted quickly to dodge the flying chips.

The boy chuckled and, pausing to wipe the sweat from his face, said, "Sure, I know how you feel. You thought we were all set for a good ole dream. Just the two of us

9

sittin' down on a log together. But it can't be done. Mrs.
Jones wants wood, an' it's our job to get it. No wood . . ."
He shrugged his shoulders to emphasize the point to
Rags. "There'd be no bread, no tucker, an' Mrs. Jones
out to see what's the matter. Not forgettin' Ross an' the
boss an' all the hungry stockmen."

Held still for the moment by the thought of the havoc he
could cause, the boy stared up at the peppercorn trees. He
could see a flock of galahs peering at him through the
drooping foliage.

"Yeah," he thought. "It's pretty right when you look at
it. No wood. No tucker. An' where do you go? When you
look at it rightly, it all swings round on me. Me an' Mrs.
Jones. An' she can't cook if I don't bring the wood."

Pleased at the way he had put himself into perspective,
the boy swung his ax again. After a heap of cut wood had
grown to considerable size, he filled the nearby wheelbarrow and trundled it to the kitchen. On his way he had to
pass through the gateway in the thick saltbush hedge.

As he let the gate bump to behind him, Alici and Maheena came around the kitchen corner. Their smooth
black faces glistened above the tops of their bright colored dresses.

"By cri'," Alici told the boy. "You late too much. Missus
say she no got 'im wood."

Stepping to one side, the two of them seemed to twine
together as they paused. The boy couldn't tell whether
they were joking or serious while they stared round-eyed
at him.

"Aw," he said, "I didn't know she was that short. You
could've got her some from the outside woodbox."

He meant the woodbox outside the kitchen where an

emergency supply of cut wood was always kept. He
glanced at the girls' dresses to see if they showed any trace
of wood grime or dust. They would have had to carry the
wood pressed against their chests. But the dresses were
unmarked.

Maheena grinned. "You look 'im all the same blackfella," she said. "Look 'im tracks." She flicked her long
black fingers down her dress and swirled with pride at its
cleanliness. "No. We no carry 'im wood, an' missus got
'im li'le bit." She held her hands together to show how
little. "But she say for you to hurry. My goodness, she say
for you to go quick time."

Clasping Alici's hand, she ran with her to the gate and
jerked it open. The two almost fell over Rags where he
lay sprawled in the dust, waiting for the boy's return. The

boy heard their squeals as he wheeled the barrow on to the kitchen.

"The trouble with them," he muttered, pushing open the door, "is the way they treat things. You don't know whether they're real or only foolin'."

Arms laden, he carried in a heap of wood to dump in the woodbox.

Mrs. Jones was at the stove pulling out some pans of steaming bread. The rich, wheaty odor made the boy's mouth water. He could taste the crust, golden brown in his mouth, as he chewed it soaked in butter.

"Cor," he said, "that smells good, Mrs. Jones. I'm sorry I let the wood run short."

He said the words slowly, not too sure that he should say them. He had noticed there was still quite a pile of billets left in the woodbox before he had dumped the other on top.

"It's like I was sayin'," he thought. "You never know with those two. Half the time they make it up as they go along."

Mrs. Jones emptied another bread tin, then closed the oven door. Her face was flushed from the heat as she turned to face the boy.

"Now what's all this you're muttering?" she asked. "And who's this might be real or only fooling?"

Smiling, she walked around the table to cut a hot, crumbly crust from the coolest loaf. As she spread it with butter, the boy pushed outside the door for another armful of wood.

"Aw," he said, coming in again, "it's just something I was thinking. The main thing is, I was talkin' about the bread. An' the wood," he added. "But the bread came first. I said it smelt good."

Mrs. Jones said, "Yes, I heard that part of it," and gave him the crust.

Squatted on the woodbox, he watched her work about the kitchen while he chewed thoughtfully, savoring the warm, crunchy bread and the rich golden butter.

"There's nothing," he thought, "that goes beyond the taste of it. Butter an' crumbs, an' the doughy part, too. If ever a feller was lucky to come to Yamboorah, I was. You don't find many around that c'n cook like Mrs. Jones."

He was sorry when the last mouthful slid down his throat and he had to finish unloading the wheelbarrow.

On his way to the door for the last time, he said, "Thanks a lot, Mrs. Jones. I'll water the chickens, then go on over to see Kanga. He's doin' a bit more to Roany's hoof today, an' he reckons I'll soon be able to ride 'im."

"Him," Mrs. Jones said, correcting. "And I'm glad. Glad Kanga has nearly cured the colt's hoof, I mean. He's a beautiful animal. But supposing he bucks when you do get on him?"

Mrs. Jones had seen some of the stockmen riding bucking horses, and it was a perpetual wonder to her how anyone could stay on such wildly contorting animals.

The boy chuckled before he let the door slam to behind him.

"Not my Roany," he told her. "Ole Kanga's gentling 'im—I mean him—at the same time as he treats the hoof. He's makin' him jus' like that big bay horse he rides himself. Almost human you might say."

Mrs. Jones nearly said that it was a pity Kanga didn't

train himself to be more human, but she changed her mind. She knew the boy saw more in the old dogman than the rock-hard dourness others might see. The two were very close, in a strange, almost silent companionship. Kanga spoke little at any time, and the boy tuned his own words in keeping. So, instead, she contented herself with a nod as the door slammed abruptly.

The boy liked to let it slide past his hip as he twisted to grab the wheelbarrow. All his movements were thought out carefully as part of the daily round. They made a pattern he had grown accustomed to.

After meeting Rags again, the boy stood the wheelbarrow on the woodheap. Wiping the last remnants of butter from his lips, he stared toward the horse yards before going to the killing pens for a bucket of water.

"You know," he told Rags as the water gushed into the big galvanized iron bucket, "where I'd sooner be is over there with ole Kanga." He nodded in the direction of the horse yards. "But he don't like no one around when he's workin'. Not even me. Though we'll slip over later to see how he's goin'."

Rags lowered one ear and swished his tail. Keen to the boy's voice, he sensed the boy was anxious; yet to his own senses the water was more important. He *knew* where the boy would be taking it.

With his nostrils close to the boy's heels, Rags followed him to the chicken pens. While the boy filled the various watering bowls, the young dog flopped in the shade of a droopy weeping willow. Lulled by the drowsy heat of midmorning, he dozed as the boy cleaned the chicken pens, then fed the squawking, clucking inmates. One, a lively young rooster, was a special favorite. The boy stroked its head before going on to the breeding pens.

Picking up two of the dozen or more fluffy yellow chicks that had been hatched the day before, the boy let them pick crushed seed from his hand. Watching their little beaks and spidery legs groping for a grip on his fingers, he marveled, as he often did, at the chicks' fragile tininess. Letting them balance on his flattened palm, he sat down contentedly.

"They c'n have a run if they want to," he told Rags. "Or scratch about round us. Won't take a minute to pop 'em back afterwards."

But the chicks stayed on the boy's hand, content to be there. And Rags closed his eyes again, content to be where he was, too, close to the boy's side.

Chicks, boy, and dog were all hunched in the tree's dappled shade when a kookaburra's laugh startled them. Perched on a limb just above, the bird sagged its big beak wide, rollicking with laughter. Disgustedly, the boy scrambled up and set the chicks back in the wire-covered pens.

"Lucky for you," he told them as they burrowed in under their mother, "that he had to laugh. If he'd kept quiet an' banged straight down—well!" He shrugged and turned away, with Rags trailing after him again. "One of you would've been his dinner."

The thought behind the words made the boy feel dejected. In his mind came a vivid picture of a golden chick, all torn and bruised, being carried away by a kookaburra. He was glad when he saw Alici and Maheena coming from the stables. Both girls talked excitedly at once when they reached him.

"We see 'im Kanga," they said. "Ride 'im colt. Ride 'im round horse yard. No got 'im limp any more."

They both pranced around in circles, stepping high-legged, to show the boy how the colt was walking. The boy watched them, choked when he saw their slim black feet stamping in the dust.

"Cor," was all he could say for a moment.

Then he led the way into the little feed shed where Rags had been born some months before and beckoned the girls to sit on the piled hay. Pulling Rags close, he squatted near them on an up-ended packing case.

"Cor," he said again. "Jus' fancy that. As a matter of fact . . ." He paused, at a loss for something to say. He wished he had been there with the girls, watching Kanga ride the colt.

Maheena nodded and sucked in her breath softly. "We savvy," she said quietly. "We savvy too much. This fella colt you love 'im true. You happy he no got 'im sore foot any more."

To ease her own feelings, Maheena stood up again to show how well the colt had walked. The boy watched her intently, and Rags peered with a puzzled expression.

Outside in the sun glare, old Kanga came from the horse yards, leading the roan colt by its reins.

Unaware of this, the boy said, "That's about it. An' you know, I'd like to have been there. Ole Kanga never says a word about what he's doin'."

He felt a feeling rising in him that he had known before, as if he were beating senselessly against the hard, implacable rock of the old dogman.

"He's always the same," the boy thought. "Though

maybe I shouldn't say that. He's done me some pretty good turns, one way an' another."

Aloud he added, "But still, he's got a right to. He's old an' knows more than any of 'em here, an' that's sayin' something." He hunched over, as if prepared to argue about the statement.

But Alici and Maheena nodded. Their rounded eyes gazed beyond the boy to the doorway, where the door sagged open on its sun-cracked leather hinges. Some inner instinct told them someone was coming, though Kanga and the colt were still out of sight, walking silently on the soft, sandy soil. Swiftly the two girls moved toward the door.

"We go now," Alici said over her shoulder. "By 'n by we see you again. Maybe tomorrow." And the two hurried, one behind the other, toward the woodheap. The boy stood up to watch them and shook his head.

"Well, I dunno," he told Rags. "Now what's got into 'em. One minute they're sittin' here on the hay an' the next minute—well, look at 'em."

He turned and glanced out of the small cobwebby window, then ran outside. Kanga was near, and the boy met him close to the little shed.

"Here y' are," Kanga said, and handed the boy the roan colt's reins. "I'm finished with 'im. Except maybe I'll look at his hoof once a month or so to see how he's goin'."

He let his hand slide once down the colt's sleek neck; then he fumbled for the pipe that bulged in his shirt pocket. As he filled the bowl with dark, coarse tobacco, he watched the boy bend down over the colt's hoof.

When Rags pressed close to see what the boy was peer-

ing at, the old dogman lit his pipe. Through the swirl of
smoke, he saw how the young dog braced its shoulders,
how its tail feathered, held close to the ground.

And the old man turned to stride slowly back to the
horse yards and beyond, to where he had his dog pack
tethered. Sight of Rags always reminded Kanga that once
the dog had been his. He had bred it to be a "king" dog but
had subsequently given the pup to the boy. Stony-faced,
the old man drew on his pipe.

But at last the boy found his voice. Though the boss had
given him the roan colt some weeks before, he had never
felt wholly sure that the colt was really his. Always in the
back of his mind lurked frightening thoughts. Kanga
might not be able to cure the hoof. The colt might yet have
to be destroyed.

Now that Kanga had said he was finished with the colt,
and that meant it was completely cured, the boy wanted
to shout and thump old Kanga on the back.

Instead, he said, "Cor, you've really fixed him, Kanga.
All that twisted frog an' everything. Why, you couldn't
tell it now from his three others."

Still wanting to do something more than just walk along
with Kanga, the boy glanced around. Rags and the sleek,
shining colt were following nose to tail. From instinct Rags
had dropped back to pad at the colt's heels.

"They're mine," the boy thought. "Two livin', shinin'
beauts. You wouldn't believe a feller could own them."

Bumping against Kanga, he almost shouted his joy before he saw the old dogman's face. The harsh, grim lines
were set in their habitual manner.

Steadied, the boy said, "I owe you a lot, Kanga. I was
tellin' that to Alici an' Maheena when you came along."

Kanga neither answered nor looked around until they reached the stables. Then he took the pipe from his mouth to say, "Keep 'im away from rocky ground for a while, an' don't go galloping him. Not for a week or two. After that, you c'n do what you like with 'im."

He spoke as if the words were forced from him. Under the tattered droop of his wide-brimmed hat, his eyes searched beyond the boy to the distant sandhills. He could see the miraged ridges dancing in the sun.

The boy said, "Yeah, I'll do that, Kanga," and knew there was nothing more to say.

Kanga's grim, tight mouth was clamped on the pipe again. His eyes had the sun-faded loneliness that was habitual to them.

"You can't change 'im," the boy thought. "No matter how you try. Though I'd give anything if he would change. Just the two of us real mates together. Talking proper, instead of this half an' half business."

He rubbed the colt's velvety nose and waited to see what Kanga would do. After the fierce sun glare, the wide stable eaves cast a cool, comfortable shadow. And listening, the boy could hear Powder and Patches, the boss's two Arab horses, stamping in their stalls. They were restless and eager to be turned out for a roll in the dust of the horse yards.

"I'm coming," he called, remembering the last words of Ross, the overseer, that morning. "Turn 'em out," he had said, "for a roll, or they'll kick the place down if the boss don't ride 'em soon."

As if suddenly remembering, Kanga strode on to where his dogs lay sprawled on the hot ground, chained to their individual pegs. All except Skipper, the pack's "king" dog, who came forward to meet the old man.

"So there you are," the boy said, leading the colt into a stall. "That's the end of Kanga for a week or two. Probably a month. Just him an' his dogs huntin' rabbits, dingoes, an' emus an' kangaroos. They say he shoots wild horses, too. I wouldn't have his job for all the money they could pay me."

Picturing old Kanga galloping after herds of wild horses with his rifle hammering viciously from his shoulder, the boy tended the colt and Powder and Patches. While the two white horses grunted and rolled in a yard, he sat down for a moment to watch the roan feed.

Rags sprawled under the feedbox, listening to the colt's teeth. To the boy it seemed that horse and dog were growing close together, as if they realized that from there onward their lives would have to be that way.

"It's funny," he thought. "But there it is. First there was me, then me an' Rags, an' now the colt. Three of us, you might say, grown from one. Just goes to show how things c'n happen."

Pleased with the thought, he brushed some straw from the colt's tail, then jerked his head for Rags to follow. Outside, they felt the hot, fierce sunlight beating on them and hurried to the little feed shed.

Wiping the sweat from his face, the boy sat down for a breather. Rags panted in the doorway. Later, when they heard a thin, piercing whistle, both went outside again to watch Kanga leave.

Tall in his saddle, the big old dogman rode eastward. Bunched behind him in tight formation trotted his pack of thirty or more dogs. Skipper, the "king" dog, padded close to the heels of the big bay horse Kanga rode. Man, horse, and dogs reminded the boy of his thoughts in the stables.

"They're together," he told Rags. "That's the secret of ole Kanga. He doesn't want anything else. Just him an' his dogs an' horse an' a great wide stretch of country to prowl around in."

When the dinner bell rang, Kanga and his dogs were nearly out of sight. Tucking in his shirt, the boy trudged slowly toward the kitchen. Passing the woodheap, he loosened his belt before pushing open the homestead gate.

"There's one thing about it," he said as he left Rags, "that's hard to understand. Ole Kanga never seems to bother whether he eats or not. If I'd have been him, I'd have stayed an' had some dinner."

Tramping swiftly around by the kitchen, he went inside. The smell of roast beef and baked pudding batter made his mouth water. For the moment at least, he was glad of the comfort they brought to him.

"You can't help it," he thought. "But you get sort of empty. It's like an ache that goes right on down inside."

Pulling back a chair, he sat down at the table. Mrs. Jones leaned over, setting down a plate; then her large white hands smoothed the cloth.

And as he ate, the boy stared out of the window. A flock of galahs screeched and fluttered somewhere beyond his vision. He wished he could see them and find out what they were squawking about, but his jaws champed steadily. Roast beef, pudding, and pumpkin soaked in gravy was his favorite dinner. The galahs could wait until the meal was over.

Chapter Two

The Search

The next morning Ross came bowleggedly through the garden gateway. Instead of his usual nod to the boy and a casual, "How are yer, son?" or, "Good day, there," he stopped to say, "I see Kanga's gone an' left the colt. You've been riding him, too, by the look of it."

Rolling a cigarette while he spoke, he lit it between cupped hands and exhaled a bluish cloud of smoke.

The boy watched it as he straightened. In its drift above Ross's head, the smoke tapered away into long, wispy fingers.

"Yeah," the boy said, leaning stiffly on his ax handle. "He's as right as anything now. I rode him yesterday afternoon."

Ross nodded. Nearby on a heap of wood chips, Rags straightened to cough warily. His hackles always bristled when the big overseer stayed to talk to the boy.

Thoughtfully, Ross said, "Well, that's fine. When this drought breaks, we'll find you some work. The pair of you, out ridin'. But at the moment take 'im easy. Each day that comes makes 'im stronger on that foot." He continued on to the horse yards, walking awkwardly.

22

Ahead of him in the horse yards, where a big mob of horses milled and snorted, the Yamboorah stockmen were saddling their mounts for the day. Over the whole familiar scene hung a reddish pall of dust. Wirranoona, an aboriginal stockman, was standing near the gates, holding the reins of two horses: one for himself, one for Ross.

"Cor," the boy thought, driving his ax into a log. "Now things are really moving. The next thing is, I'll be walkin' bowlegged like the rest of 'em."

To accentuate the thought, he walked around with his legs straddled while he gathered wood and dumped it in the wheelbarrow. Ted, the odd-job man, saw him from the garden gateway.

"So help me," he called to the boy. "Now what's got into you? You look like a duck that's got rheumatism."

Chuckling, he pushed the gate open and shut several times while he examined the hinges. Then he poured oil on them from a can he carried.

The boy said, "Aw, I sort of felt stiff in the legs."

He trundled the barrow forward, and Ted held the gate open for him. As the boy went through, Ted squirted some oil on the barrow's squeaking wheel.

"That'll fix that," he said, meaning the squeak. "But goanna oil's best for yourself. I allus use it for a twinge or an ache." Then he added, "I'll be cuttin' a bit of chaff an' could do with a hand. Come on over if yer get the chance."

The boy said, "Thanks, Ted, I will. I reckon I ought now there's a horse of my own to feed," and wheeled the barrow on around to the kitchen.

Ted swung the gate open and shut for two or three more times, then went on toward the stables.

"He's a funny kid," he muttered to himself. "But you can't help liking him. Him an' that dog make a darn good pair."

Later, after a big mound of silvery-gold chaff had been cut, Ted cleaned and oiled the chaffcutter. The boy, with Rags at his heels, trudged off to search for eggs under the big saltbush hedge.

Passing a stall, boy and dog went in for the fourth time that morning to stare at the roan colt.

"He's a beaut," the boy told Rags while he smoothed the colt's neck. "But we've got to watch him. Keep 'im away, like Kanga says, from rocks an' stones."

He was bent over the colt's hoof when the boss came in. Rags's warning growl made the boy spin around quickly. The colt snorted and jumped away, startled by the movement.

The boss smiled. "Well! Well! Well!" he said. "All together, eh? I had a feeling I'd find you here." He scratched his chin in a slow, thoughtful way, then added, "Now he's right, an' eating his head off, you might as well ride him. Canter out to the Ten Mile bore an' see if the mill is pumping. While you're there, clean the trough."

Knowing the boy had no idea where the Ten Mile bore was, the boss took him outside and drew a map of a small part of Yamboorah in the dust. With his finger he scratched a meandering line indicating the track the boy was to follow.

"You branch off the main track about two miles east," the boss said. "Then turn southeast. You can't miss it."

He spoke with the familiarity of a man who was born on the thousand square miles of country he owned. There were areas of worthless or unused land that he did not

know well, but he knew every inch of the tracks that criss-
crossed Yamboorah.

The boy nodded, puzzled by the drawing. His eyes
glanced eastward as he straightened.

"Two miles," he thought. "How d' you know when
you've gone two miles, just joggin' along on a horse? There
must be all sorts of tracks runnin' everywhere."

Glancing around to the boss again, he said, "Yeah. I'll
find it. An' if the mill's not pumpin', what do I do?"

"Nothing," the boss said. "Just come back an' tell me,
an' I'll send Ted out to fix it. Or maybe one of the others.
O.K., then, see that you get moving."

He turned away, and the boy, suddenly remembering,
called, "Er, I was just goin' to gather the eggs. Mrs.
Jones'll be needin' some this afternoon."

The boss stopped long enough to say, "You'll be back
by then, in time to gather 'em. I'll tell her though, you
might be late for your dinner."

He continued on his way, shading his eyes with his hand
while he stared toward the shimmering sandhills that
stretched westward. The boy went inside the stall again to
saddle the roan.

Riding it out under the broad, shading eaves, he thrilled
to the colt's springy movement. It seemed to him that the
colt had four well-oiled springs instead of just four ordi-
nary legs.

"Cor," he said down to Rags as they passed under the
big old peppercorn trees. "You ought to be up here. It's
like having padded silk movin' along under you."

He stretched his legs in the stirrups and settled comfort-
ably. His free hand reached to stroke the roan's neck.

Down in the dust stirred by the colt's hoofs, Rags followed quietly, ears pricked to the boy's voice. Above, in the peppercorn trees, galahs squawked their usual chorus. The boy could see some of them peering down at him. Their rosy breasts and pale gray wings bobbed like flowers through the leaves.

"Of all the birds," the boy said, looking up, "you're about the noisiest. Though maybe the kookaburras ain't far behind."

Beyond again, as he left the trees behind, he could see two kookaburras wrestling in mid-air. They were squabbling over a lizard that was locked in both their beaks.

"I dunno," the boy said, more to himself than Rags or the colt. "There's always some sort of trouble. An' of that lot, the lizard's got the worst. Yet nobody bothers. Scaly-backed horrors, Mrs. Jones calls 'em. But they're alive, like the rest of us. An' that fella's gettin' torn in two."

Baffled as always by the rip and claw of nature, he rode on, trying to solve the cruelty or formulate the reason for it.

His mind groped to find another way for all birds and animals to be fed, until at last he said, "There isn't any. Whichever way you go, there's no way out. Even cabbages an' grass are alive if you want to eat 'em. They must be, or they wouldn't grow an' die."

Then his thoughts changed. He sighted three kangaroos hopping along in the distance. They were red ones, big and sleek in the bright morning sunlight. As yet the day had stayed fairly cool with a fresh southerly wind blowing. Watching the 'roos, the boy saw them bound out of sight behind a straggling scrub clump.

Later, when he reached the faint track he thought must

be the one that led to the Ten Mile, he saw traces of them again. This time it was their pad and tail marks vividly printed in the dust ahead of him.

"Oh, ho," he thought. "We're all goin' the same way. Maybe they're thirsty an' heading for a drink."

Pleased at the thought, he nudged the colt and urged him into a canter. Rags loped behind, keeping pace with the colt's rhythm.

Soon the boy saw the big red bodies bounding along ahead. They were leaping, now clear of all scrub, across a wide sweep of plain. The track ran straight, like twin ribbons scarred in the dry red earth. For a moment the boy was tempted to gallop after the flying forms, but he changed his mind, remembering what Kanga had said.

"It'd be great," he told the roan colt, "to really rip along after 'em. But we're not goin' to. That hoof of yours has got to take it easy."

Fresh from its weeks in the stalls, the colt wanted to gallop. Rags, too, whined in eagerness for the chase. His whole body danced, vibrant with excitement.

The boy steadied colt and dog with his hands and voice, then relaxed again in the saddle. Shading his eyes, he watched the 'roos bound on into the distance. They seemed to be full of a ghostly, quiet dignity as they leaped with silent movement. No whisper of sound came from their pads and tails.

"They're all steel an' balance," he thought. "The tail seems to hit, yet it don't. Just holds 'em steady for another great leap."

After the 'roos had disappeared, merged in the scrub ahead, he kept his gaze searching for the windmill. When

it showed, the galvanized iron sails were glinting brightly. Some big bony cows with calves at foot were drinking at the trough. Amongst them the boy noticed the three red kangaroos sitting still on their haunches. Their backs were to him, and they were contentedly wiping their muzzles.

"Well, there you are," he said, and reined the colt down to a slow walk. "You all look full to the whiskers."

As some of the cows were still drinking, he stopped the colt altogether, so as not to disturb them.

"Let 'em have their fill," he told the roan. "Then we c'n go close. It won't matter then if they do get cranky an' bolt away."

He sat quietly until one of the cows raised her long-horned head and saw him. He was scared for a moment. Snorting a call to her calf, she ran straight toward him, then suddenly veered away. Behind her high-tailed rump, the calf kicked and capered. As if drawn by a magnet,

the rest followed suit, including the three kangaroos. In
a bawling, jumping, twisting circle, they raced around
the boy before they disappeared into some nearby scrub.
Head to tail with the cattle, the kangaroos leaped errati-
cally.

"Cor," the boy said, and let the excited roan prance toward the trough. "Can you beat that? Kangaroos, cows,
an' calves all kickin' around together! For a minute, I
thought they were goin' to run right over me."

He slid from the colt and tied him to a nearby tree.
Rags joined him then for a tour around the big windmill
tower, the enormous galvanized iron water tank, and the
fifty-foot-long trough.

"Everything seems all right," the boy said after he had
climbed up to peer into the great tank. "It's full of water,
an' so is the trough. The mill's pumpin', too. There's a fair
ole stream comin' out of that pipe." He meant the long
overhead pipe that carried the water from the mill pump-
rod casing across to the great holding tank.

The boy was interested in mills. He liked their heights
and their depths.

"This one," he thought, "is about a forty-foot tower,
with a fourteen-foot span of sails."

He scrambled between the metal struts of the tower
and tapped the bore-casing. "An' down below, she's bored
about three hundred and fifty feet into the ground—or so
Ted said. That's a long way when you think of it, though
some of 'em go deeper. Two or three times that, I've
heard."

Wondering what the earth was like at that depth, he
shivered in the hot sun glare.

"Uhh!" he said to Rags. "All that cold wet earth pressing on yer. Black, too, as the inside of a box with the lid shut. You remember that time when the feedbin lid fell shut on me?" It had been dark then, he vividly remembered. Blacker than any night when the stars were covered.

Rags listened to the boy but made no sign or whimper. He was content to have the boy back on the ground with him. When the boy rode the colt, there was a gulf between them that Rags did not like. He liked best the smell of the boy's tight, sun-cracked boots in front of him—not the lively, jigging heels of the colt.

The boy sensed some of this as the young dog glanced up at him. There was a softness in its eyes that mirrored more than words.

Reaching down, the boy said, "Come on, feller. We'll pretend you're little. I'll carry you over an' dump you in the trough."

With Rags thrown onto his shoulder, he climbed out between the struts again and trudged toward the trough. Then he saw two emus coming in to drink. Shy and wary, they came with short, high-stepping strides that seemed to hold their scaly legs and claws hovering in the air. Yet for some reason they did not appear unduly worried by sight of the boy, except that they stretched their necks higher to stare at him unwinkingly.

Changing his mind, the boy crept away to hide behind the tree where the colt was tied. Unconscious of the vast loneliness around him, in which countless emus must have been nesting or feeding, he was conscious only of the two coming in to water.

As he lowered Rags, he whispered, "Now don't make a

noise. Let 'em drink an' enjoy it. We'll scout around after-wards an' look for some eggs. Ole Ross said once they're good for cakes. Maybe Mrs. Jones c'n try 'em.''

Absorbed in a picture of himself carrying a great sack-ful of emu eggs, he watched the emus drink. Stretching out their necks, they scooped a beakful of water, then tipped up their heads to let the water run down their long, thin gullets.

"It's got a long way to go," the boy thought. "An' they can't do it in a hurry. Got to let it slide down, little by lit-tle.''

And his thoughts changed then to their wings as the male bird suddenly plunged its head right under water and flapped its wings in ecstasy.

"They're too small,'' the boy told Rags. "They couldn't fly an inch in 'em. They don't even use 'em to scuttle along the ground.''

Seeing that Rags looked puzzled, the boy chuckled. He liked to think sometimes that the dog really understood what he was saying. It added, he thought, to the interest of the conversation.

"Yeah,'' he added, "you're not the only one. I heard Ross saying they're old. They go right back to the time when no birds could fly. It's funny, though, how they never caught up. You'd reckon if other birds could grow wings, they could. They'd be a pretty fair sight flyin' around up there.''

Lost completely in his thoughts, he stood up swiftly to wave his arm at the sky. Startled into action, the emus plunged straight over the trough in a leggy, floundering jump, then pounded away in their peculiar rocking trot that had the speed of a galloping horse. The boy stared after them, shading his eyes.

After a time, he said, "Oh well, that's that. They had a good drink while they were here. Now I'd better clean the trough. What with one thing an' another, it'll never get done."

Under the trough, near the plug hole, he found a big broom. Every watering point on Yamboorah had one, so that the troughs could be kept clean. Before he unscrewed the plug, the boy wedged up the ball cock.

"That'll stop the water," he told Rags, "until I do the first sweep. Then we c'n let some run to make a final rinse. Leave it sweet an' shiny bright. Not like it is now, all green with scum."

Kicking off his boots and rolling up his trousers, he climbed into the trough. Shin-deep at first in the slowly draining water, he scrubbed with the broom at the sides and bottom. Soon the water slopped and swirled, green with scum, as he worked contentedly. To clean a trough was one of his favorite jobs. He liked to see afterward the sheen of clean, glittering water sparkling in the trough's cleanliness. He imagined horses and cattle coming in for a drink and enjoying it all the more.

"It must be great," he thought, "to suck the stuff in an' let it trickle out through yer nose. Sort of clean an' restful like, especially when the water's clear."

For a final rinse, he slapped up and down the trough, brooming the now almost clear water. Rags splashed with him, every so often shaking off a spray of water that sparkled in the sun. When at last the boy screwed down

the plug in the plug hole, the galvanized iron of the
trough was immaculate.

"Lovely," he said, and hopped around on one foot, putting on a boot. "You could see your face in it now if you
wanted to."

With both boots stamped firmly on to his feet again, he
prepared to mount the roan. In the distance, as he put one
foot into a stirrup, he noticed two horses swirling a stream
of dust behind them. From the whitish blur they made
against the red dust, he knew they were Powder and
Patches. The two dark figures on their backs, he guessed,
were Alici and Maheena.

"Now what," he wondered thoughtfully, riding the roan
toward them, "do they want? The boss must've sent 'em or
they wouldn't be ridin' his horses."

Lately, the boss spent a lot of time in his office or driving in a car. Since the two girls had come to work on Yamboorah, he often let them exercise his horses.

"They eat their heads off," the boy had heard him tell
Ross, "an' get too toey. If the girls ride 'em, it lets off a bit
of steam."

And Ross had nodded, gazing into the distance. His
brown craggy face mirrored the same anxiety that was
almost always on the boss's. Both men peered constantly,
searching the sky for signs of rain.

When the girls drew close, the boy saw they were dressed
in men's trousers and shirts. Their bare feet just showed,
resting lightly in the stirrups. Both had their long black
hair tied back with a piece of ribbon.

"That's Mrs. Jones," he thought. "She likes to see 'em
done up a bit one way or another. Like telling me to wash
or put a comb through my hair."

Unconsciously, he rubbed his head. The hair felt bleached and dry, scorched by the sun. Dusty, too, under the quick, light brush of his fingers.

As if knowing his thoughts, Alici said, "Plenty dust. We need 'im rain too much. That last big fella storm not enough. Poof! He dry away finish." She waved her free hand, cupping it up toward the sky.

The boy nodded. Memory of the big storm, which had doused a roaring stretch of bushfire, came to him. For a moment both the rain and fire seemed to be beating on his shoulders.

Shaking his tousled head, he said, "Yeah, you'd think it would have gone deeper. Into the ground, I mean. Instead, in a couple of days it was dried out. Finished." He waved his hand in a similar way to Alici—a habit he had of copying when talking to other people.

Maheena said, "Yes. 'Im all the same true. Me savvy this dust for choke 'im." She opened her mouth as if she were gasping, and the boy saw her pinkish tongue, edged by snowy, glistening teeth. "More better," she added after gulping quickly, "we drink along windmill first time. After that, we talk 'im li'le bit. Tell 'im you something."

The boy said, "Sure! I was thirsty m'self when I got here, so I reckon you two must be."

Reining the roan around, he cantered it abreast of Powder and Patches as the two bounded forward, scenting the water.

Alici and Maheena flashed their teeth in excited smiles, shortening their reins, ready for a race. But the boy checked them.

Jabbing downward with his finger, he shouted, "Don't forget his leg. Got to take 'im easy, ole Kanga said."

The two girls straightened, then eased their horses to a trot.

"Head belong we two," Maheena called, leaning over toward the boy, "all the same wood. Got 'im no brain for savvy 'im anything."

The boy shouted back, "Aw, go on. You're a couple of good 'uns most times. I nearly forgot m'self, this mornin'."

At the trough the girls slid from their saddles while Powder and Patches drank. Taking first turn, Maheena bent over to drink fresh, gushing water from the inlet pipe, while Alici pushed down the ball cock. Then the two reversed the procedure. Both had dripping chins and wet, straggly hair when they climbed back into their saddles.

"Now," Maheena said, scuffing a hand across her mouth, "we can talk." And she went on to tell the boy why the boss had sent them.

He, the boss—after the boy had left—had had one of his restless spasms. Climbing the homestead windmill tower to scan the horizon with his field glasses, he had seen a thin column of smoke. Someone was camped on the southernmost edges of the sandhills.

"He say," Maheena ended by saying, "that we go look 'im. We two fella"—she tapped her own chest, then Alici's—"because we savvy all this country. You fella"—she touched the boy's arm—"for learn 'im. For learn 'im everything about this place, Yamboorah." The word sounded different mouthed gutturally through her lips.

The boy stared. In the thoughts jumbling up through his mind, he seemed to be growing. His shoulders were as wide and flat as old Kanga's.

Trying to speak normally, he said, "Yeah! Well! We c'n soon do that."

Then he shaded his eyes to gaze beyond the windmill, and beyond again to where he judged the southern edges of the sandhills must lie. But mile after mile of scrub and plains lay in between.

"About where," he asked, "do you reckon to head? I mean about where do you reckon he said the smoke was?"

And in the asking, he felt he was shrinking again. "They *know*," he thought. "An' I don't. They c'n ride straight across as if there was a road cut for 'em to follow."

Both girls pointed at once. Their slim black fingers gestured in the same direction.

"Dis way," Alici said. "Long way li'le bit, but no matter." She slapped the saddlebag strapped to her saddle. "We got 'im samwich. Got 'im billy, too, for make 'im tea."

The boy had already noticed the bulging saddlebags both girls had buckled to their saddles. Alici also had a billycan strapped to the cantle dees, and Maheena had a water bag slung around Patches' neck. He guessed that it held rainwater from one of the kitchen tanks. Rainwater made better tea than the slightly brackish water from the bore.

Nodding slowly, he said, "O.K. then. You lead, an' I'll follow. But remember Roany's hoof. Don't go too fast on the rocky places."

Riding abreast, one each side of the boy, the girls held their mounts steady with the roan. All three horses were good walkers and strode along stride for stride. Rags trotted behind, content with the steady, mile-covering pace.

At varying times the boy felt one of the girls shouldering her horse against the roan, bumping against it for a second or two.

"They're keepin' me in line," he thought. "An' doin' it

their way. No, not over there, or here, sort of thing, but jus' pokin' along nice an' steady. That's why they won't ride out in the lead. They want me to feel I'm as wide awake as they are in findin' the direction."

Around noon, when the shade was small under the scrubby trees, they made a midday camp. The boy gathered wood for a fire that Maheena lit; then the three squatted down, waiting for the billy to boil.

Later, after the sandwiches were eaten and the last dregs of tea drained, the boy wiped his mouth.

Sitting back on his heels, he said, "That was great. Mrs. Jones sure knows how to make a good san'wich. You c'n taste the meat mixin' with the bread." He licked his lips, tasting the crumbs that still lingered.

Alici said, "Yers, good too much. S'pose me got 'im 'nother one me eat 'im, too."

Her glance wistfully followed the wrapping paper Maheena folded and stowed in her saddlebag. She wished the paper was still full with another great mound of sandwiches.

Seeing the glance, Maheena said, "By 'n by you fat like anything." She gestured with her hands. "Li'le bit stomach grow into big bit, then where you stop? S'pose 'im you too big you no fit for ride 'im horse." She looked at the boy as if asking him to agree with her.

The boy nodded, yet wanted to be impartial. He felt that another sandwich or two wouldn't have made much difference. Alici looked as slim as a sapling stripped of its leaves after a big wind.

"Yeah," he said. "You might be right. But I don't reckon we ate all that much. Just about right I'd say, allowin' for an odd bite or two. Mrs. Jones ain't ever far out when it comes to servin' tucker."

He had a vision for a moment of Mrs. Jones in the kitchen putting food on his plate. He could almost smell the savor of the meat and gravy.

The two girls laughed. Light on their bare feet, they reached for their reins. As they swung up into their saddles, the boy followed suit, though he was slower in his movements. His boots always felt stiff and too tight for his feet after he had been sitting still for a while. A chuckle wrinkled the freckles around his eyes as he nudged the roan with his heel.

"Me an' my boots," he told the girls, "are always late. You beat me every time on those bare feet of your'n. The trouble is, I need a new pair." He stared down fleetingly at his booted feet, braced each side of Roany. "Another two sizes larger, I'd reckon, to get a good fit."

Alici said, "Yers, you want 'im big some more. By an' by, me buy 'im shoes, too. All the same missus." She pushed a foot forward so she could see her bare toes braced on the stirrup iron.

The boy shook his head. He liked riding along talking to the two girls. There was a kind of quietness in their voices that suited the great Bush distances—as if they were tuned to the dwarfing vastness.

"No," he said. "I wouldn't, if I was you. You're happy like you are, an' you stay that way. Take me," he added. "I'm always in strife. Especially early. I can't get 'em on, sometimes." And he explained in detail the things he had to do some mornings to get the boots on.

The girls listened absorbedly, yet stared ahead, search-

ing the skyline. No trace of smoke showed against the
hazed, glaring shimmer, and after riding for an hour or
more, Maheena whispered, as if to herself, "Dis fella light
'im fire gone. Gone altogether die away finis'. No see 'im
someplace any more." She sighed and shaded her eyes for
a final look toward the sandhills, which were now in full
view.

Alici said, "S'pose 'em we circle round li'le bit; maybe
we find 'em something. See 'im track maybe."

As with Maheena, there was no doubt in her voice. Both
girls were certain they were in the area where the boss had
seen the campfire burning.

Nudging their horses, the two changed course to ride in
a great circle, while the boy followed.

"How do they do it?" he thought, reining the roan in
check. "Just a puff of smoke all them miles away, an' here
we are, right on the spot. Or so they say. An' I'll bet we
are. Somewhere here we'll find the ashes."

The thought was barely in his mind when Maheena slid
from her saddle. Squatting down, she scraped at the dust
until the grayish powder of wood ash filtered through her
fingers.

Standing upright again, she said, "Blackfella camp.
Three, maybe four fella"—she held up the fingers of her
hand—"stop along dis place."

Alici rode beyond her to a pad of footmarks in the dust
and followed them for a little way. When she came back,
her eyes were bright with the knowledge she had learned.

"Three fella buck an' two fella lubra," she said, holding
up her hand to show Maheena, then the boy. "They cass'
'im something. Carry 'im all the same dis." She humped

over, gripping both hands as if she were carrying a load
on her shoulders.

The boy said, "I can understand you knowing there
were three men an' two women. An' that the fire was an
abo's by the way they've covered the ashes. But about 'em
catchin' something, an' carryin' whatever it was, that's got
me beat."

It seemed to him that kangaroos would be the logical
thing for the aborigines to carry, though he suddenly remembered that he hadn't noticed any recent kangaroo
tracks.

"Cor," he thought. "I'm just tryin' to let on that I know
a bit myself, an' I don't. A few tracks on the ground is as
far as I c'n see. Not read the whole story like they do."

Maheena said, "No! No carry 'im kangaroo. Carry 'im
something me by 'n by savvy."

Balanced on tiptoes, she walked about slowly, studying
the ground. Suddenly, she whirled and hurried back to
her horse.

"Got 'im now," she added, climbing up into her
saddle. "They carry 'im eggs. Emu eggs. They gather 'em dis place an' pile 'em up there." She pointed
down to where she had suddenly turned. The boy saw
only a patch of barely disturbed dust.

But Alici said, "Plenty eggs. Plenty too much. That's
why they take 'em go 'long sandhills."

She gestured toward the edge of the brooding sandhills,
then rode close to Maheena. Knee to knee, the two girls
nudged their horses. Ahead stretched the plains and scrub-
lands between them and Yamboorah homestead.

Urging the roan after them, the boy said, "That's a bit

mad, ain't it? Goin' into the sandhills. They could die out there in that desert. It nearly killed me one time."

He looked around as he spoke, and his mind was full of a memory. Rags was trotting behind in his accustomed place, and the boy remembered being lost in the sandhills; he and the dog gasping up one slithery slope after another, and the terrible sameness that smothered them. And the final heat-seared memory of groveling for shade from the sun.

He shivered as he added, "Didn't we ought to sort of do something about 'em? Go after 'em an' see how they are?"

He knew they were two silly questions but felt he had to ask them. The memory for the moment overshadowed what he knew most aborigines could endure.

Maheena said, "Blackfella dance for bring 'im rain." Her eyes rolled, showing a vague, uneasy fear. "More better now we no look further. This not good dance for boy an' girl to see."

She stared around quickly, as if expecting that something frightening could spring upon her.

The boy saw her fear. Alici, too, was tense.

"All right," the boy said. "We'll leave 'em to it."

Nudging the roan between the girls' two horses again, he was silent for several minutes before saying, "But why out there in all that sand? You'd reckon they'd pick a better place near water or something."

As if painted in front of his eyes, he saw a picture of aboriginal men and women dancing in a grassy hollow. Their black, lean figures stood out sharply against the green.

Alici whispered, "By 'n by finis'. Sand lose 'im everything. No see 'im tracks, nothing. You savvy that?" She leaned over in her saddle and peered so closely into the boy's face that her nose brushed his cheek. "You savvy 'im why no see 'im nothing?" She smoothed with her hand, leveling imaginary sand.

The boy nodded. "Yeah," he whispered. "I savvy. The wind comes along blowin' the sand an' covers the tracks of what they've been up to. Though I tell you this," he added aloud, "I don't believe in 'em, whatever they are. The tricks, I mean. You can't *make* rain come, whatever you do. Now come on. See if we c'n find some eggs for Mrs. Jones. They're good for cookin', ain't they?"

Both girls smiled. Relieved from the swift tension that had built in their minds, they began to ride more freely. Their hands fluttered in their habitual gestures.

"Sure," mimicked Maheena, "we find 'im some. We find 'im plenty. Me all the time carry sugar bag along dis place." She patted one of the saddlebags strapped to her saddle.

The boy said, "Fine! Let's look for 'em then," and the three reined their horses toward a stretch of denser scrub. Soon they were in amongst groves of thin, spindly saplings, which cast a network of dappled shadow.

Suddenly, both saplings and their shadows began to tremble as big, heavy shapes pounded through them. It seemed to the boy that there was a great flock of emus flooding through the scrub, though in reality there were no more than about twenty. The long-necked, trotting birds scurried past or away, in irregular, darting movements. Their gangling legs seemed unequal to their long, top-heavy bodies as the boy stopped in astonishment.

But Alici and Maheena slid from their saddles and tied Powder and Patches to a strong sapling.

"Queek," Alici shouted. "By 'n by maybe come back, peck 'im head belong we fella." She tapped her head as she ran to show the boy what she meant.

Imagining himself being struck on the head by a horde of angry emus while he struggled in the midst of them, the boy swung down to help. Running stiffly in his boots, with Rags at his heels, he followed the two girls deeper in amongst the saplings. Striding crazily, he leaped headlong over a log and fell into a hollow. Almost under his chest were three green emu eggs, bunched neatly in the dust.

"Hey!" he shouted. "There's three of 'em here," and in his haste scooped them up in an armful. Through the scrub he could see both girls bending down.

Maheena shouted for him to, "Bring 'em come queek; we get 'em plenty this place."

Then he glanced over his shoulder to see a string of emus trotting back. Their heads were bobbing angrily on their weaving, storklike necks.

Grabbing the reins of all three horses, the boy shouted, "They're comin' back. A dozen of 'em all in a line. I've got your horses if yer hurry."

He tried to lead the horses through the scrub, but their reins and stirrups got tangled in the saplings.

From somewhere that seemed to him to be far, far away, he heard both girls shouting, "Take off your shirt. Take off your shirt. Take off your shirt an' lie down someplace for wave 'im. Wave 'im slow for all the same make 'em flutter."

The boy said, "Cor!" and felt the sweat bead on his neck.

Yet he moved mechanically. First he tied the horses to a sapling again, then ripped off his shirt. Running toward the emus and sprawling flat on his back, he waved the shirt around in a slow, circling motion. Rags sank by the boy's side, baffled by the procedure.

One after the other the emus bumped together as they came to a stop, then stepped haltingly to peer at the boy's shirt. As if mesmerized, they began to bob and sway while they slowly edged nearer. Rags snarled at them softly, wrinkling his lips.

To the boy lying stiffly on the ground, the emus seemed enormous—all scaly legs and big, steely claws. He wanted to jump up again and run, run, run.

But he heard Maheena shouting, "Close up finis', now we got 'im sackful. We bring 'em horse when everything right."

He guessed she meant when she had mounted with the eggs or untangled the horses from where he had left them.

"They'll hurry," he thought, "but it ain't too good down here. Those emus' feet are gettin' closer an' closer."

Sweating all over now, he kept the shirt moving. Under his shoulders he felt the twigs and gravelly dust biting into his skin. The emus were so close that he was looking up at their featherless bellies when at last Alici rode near, leading Roany. The emus surged away, startled out of their semi-trance, and the boy scrambled up.

"Come on, Rags!" he yelled. "We've had enough of this."

But as the boy swung into his saddle, Rags suddenly lost all control and raced after the big birds. They stopped as one and wheeled in tight formation. To the shouting boy and screaming girl, it seemed as if Rags had plunged into a forest of scaly legs. The next moment the dog shot high in the air, kicked by a hard, clawed foot.

Rags landed on his paws, then crouched to plunge at the emus again.

Jumping the roan forward, the boy shouted, "Come out of it, Rags, or they'll kill you. You ought t' have more sense."

Though he turned to obey, Rags snarled angrily. The boy guessed he was mad at being bullied by the emus. Their bold, snaky heads and mincing, curious steps had somehow shown contempt.

"It's the huntin' instinct in 'em," the boy thought, even while he shouted again, "Come on out of it before they kick your head off."

By then Rags was close to Roany's heels, and the boy heard Alici shout, "Quick time now. Maheena gone with eggs. We catch 'er someplace." Bent low over her horse's neck, she ducked and weaved through the scrub, while the boy followed.

Reaching a stretch of plains country, they saw Maheena just ahead, riding slowly, as she balanced her sugar sack filled with eggs.

"By cri'," she said to the boy and Alici when they rode near. "We got 'im plenty. Missus Jones gon' be pleased too much."

The boy said, "Yeah," and pulled on his shirt. He could still feel the dust and twigs clinging to his back. "But what about the boss? What are we gonna tell 'im about what's been happenin'?"

"Tell 'im we see 'im blackfella tracks," Alici said. "Tell

'im true about what we see." She waved her hands toward the desert lands. "Blackfella gone for make 'im corroboree."

"True," said Maheena. "He savvy 'im everything belong we fella. Perhaps by 'n by," she added, "you help me carry eggs. They heavy like anything in this sack." She had the full sack in front of her, balanced on the pommel.

"Sure," the boy said. "I'll take it now."

For the rest of the journey home to Yamboorah, the three were silent. Rags trotted behind, hidden almost by the drifting dust.

And later, after the horses had been washed and fed and Alici and Maheena had gone to talk with the boss, the boy bumped his way into the kitchen. Mrs. Jones was in the pantry, seaching among the jars on a shelf.

"My goodness!" she said when she came out. "What on earth have you there? Are they some kind of pumpkin or something?" She stared at the sack the boy was lowering.

"No," he said. "Eggs. We reckoned you might like 'em. They're good for cookin', an' . . . an' . . ." He shrugged, baffled by whatever else the eggs might be good for.

Mrs. Jones lifted an egg, then another. Even in her large, capable hands, the eggs looked enormous. Very carefully, she turned away from the boy so that he couldn't see her face.

"Whatever shall I do with them?" she thought as she set the eggs on the table. "I'd need a hammer to break them. And besides, you never know what might drop out."

Turning around again, she said, "They're lovely, but of

course very strange. I'll have to ask Ross or someone how to use them."

"Sure," the boy said, and rubbed his head happily. "He'll tell you that, an' so will some of the others. I'll bet you, Mrs. Jones, they'll make great cakes. An' be great, I reckon, for some brownie." He meant the big brown cakes, dotted with raisins, that Mrs. Jones baked in large, flat tins.

"I'll bet they will," Mrs. Jones told him. "Now put them in the pantry while we have a cup of tea. You can tell me what sort of a day you've had while I prepare the dinner."

That night the boy sprawled on his bunk with Rags curled at his feet. Outside in the moonlit hedgerow, a rooster stirred, flapping its wings. Somewhere beyond the killing pens, a mopoke called.

"It was a good day," the boy muttered, and yawned tiredly. "An' it was good about those emus. They were nearly dancin' on my head, yet never touched me. Just goes to show that those two girls know a thing or two."

He went to sleep merged in a haze of scaly legs. Rags snuffled at his feet, dreaming his own dreams of the leg that had kicked him.

Chapter Three

Ted Welds a Buggy Wheel Tire

For several days the boy trudged around in his usual routine: feeding the three stabled horses, cutting wood, gathering eggs, and doing the varying odd jobs that Ross or Mrs. Jones gave him.

One afternoon he was squatting on a log, sharpening his ax with a file, when the boss rode by on Patches. Behind the boy, Rags lay in the shade of one of the many logs piled on the woodheap.

"Good day there, son," the boss said. "I see you're puttin' an edge on it." He nodded at the ax gripped between the boy's knees. "I like to see tools kept an eye on. They tell me you got around all right the other day. Found your way all right an' picked up some tracks, as well as an egg or two."

His smooth brown face wrinkled for a moment when he chuckled. Yet his eyes held the quiet, steady gaze that the boy felt could see right through him.

"Yeah," the boy said, and tested the ax edge carefully by rubbing his thumb along it. "But it wasn't really me. Those two girls did most of the findin'." Wiping his

49

thumb on his trousers, he bent over with the file again.

"That's how you learn," the boss said. "An' what I wanted. It takes a long time to get the feel of Yamboorah." As he gathered his reins, he added, "How did the eggs go? Did Mrs. Jones use 'em?"

"Sure," the boy said. "Lovely. Ted cracked 'em for her with a hammer, an' she made a batch of brownie. Just a few, of course. She's still got a whackin' great heap of 'em left in the pantry."

While he was speaking, his eyes could see the eggs bulging in their sugar bag on the floor.

"It's Alici an' Maheena," he thought. "If they get something, they get a lot. Eggs, honey, it don't matter. They like t' see full an' plenty."

Aloud, he went on to say, "But they'll be all right there. Ted says they'll keep for weeks, even in this heat." He wiped his sweaty face to add emphasis.

"Yes," the boss agreed. "Let's hope some rain comes soon. If it doesn't, there'll be a great roarin' bushfire—one that'll burn us right out. Not like that other little caper."

He meant the short, sudden bushfire caused by a storm some month or so earlier. It had nearly cost the lives of himself, the boy, Alici, Maheena, the roan colt, and Rags. The boss still had the faint burn scars on his face and neck.

"Yers," the boy said, and looked away. Among his memories, the searing, tearing fire was the most frightening. Or was it? Maybe even worse was the time he had run away to cross the sandhills.

Watching him, the boss saw the memories flooding the boy's eyes. They clouded as if fearing, yet glad of the memories.

"So there it is," the boss thought. "That's what it's like to be young—or a young 'un like him. The whole world's a dream, yet a real, tough one that has to be faced."

Nudging Patches with his spurs, the boss said, "Well, I'll leave you to it. Give Ted a hand later over at the forge —but don't get into any trouble. You have to learn, though it doesn't always have to be the hard way."

He left on the skittering, dancing horse, and the boy heard his chuckle. There was a kind of warmth in the sound that made him happy. He felt like throwing the ax in the air.

"No," he shouted. "Jus' leave it to me. I'm the best off-sider ole Ted ever had."

Driving the ax into a log, he watched the boss for a moment. Horse and rider were part of the vast brown landscape that the boy loved so well. He could see beyond and around for what seemed endless distances.

"This is me," he thought. "Standin' here. But I'm out there, really. In the whole of it, to where there ain't no ending."

"Pleased at the way he had shaped the thought, he beckoned Rags to follow. The two went first to the little feed shed, then on toward the stables.

"We'll have a look at Roany first," the boy told Rags, "an' see how he's doin'. Then go on to Ted. I c'n hear 'im beltin' at something over there in the forge. If I remember rightly, he's puttin' a rim on a wheel. One of them on the buggy the boss is havin' fixed."

While he walked, the boy thought over what he had said. Nobody ever seemed to tell him directly what was happening on Yamboorah, yet by some means or other he always

knew. Not always directly, but in roundabout ways that filtered through to him; either in what he overheard or in
preparations he saw being made.

"It's funny when you think," he told Rags, inside the stables. "Yet I s'pose it's right. You couldn't expect 'em to
come round tellin' *me* just what's goin' on. To them I'm
the boy that chops a bit of wood an' slops about with a
bucket or two of water. Yet there'd be a moan if I wasn't
here to do it."

Seeing all the trouble involved if he wasn't there to do his
job, the boy went into Roany's stall. Rags stayed at the
door, content to watch the boy fondle the colt's glossy neck,
then walk around admiringly. It was a pattern of movement the dog had seen so many times that it had now lost
its interest.

"Yeah," the boy said, bending down, "that hoof is good.
Sound as a bell that ain't got a crack in it. Next time old
Kanga's in, he won't have a thing to do, except maybe
change the shoe."

Thinking of the old dogman, he went outside again,
after giving the colt a final rub.

"He's due home soon," the boy told Rags as they headed
for the blacksmith's shop. "An' when he gets here, I'll bet
he'll be pleased. You can't get away from it. I've
taken good care of Roany. No galloping 'im or bumpin'
him on stony ground."

He said it with pride, remembering Kanga's instructions. Rags sniffed and flicked a fly from one twitching
ear. He sensed that the boy was pleased by the tone of his
murmuring voice.

In the blacksmith's shop, Ted leaned over the forge,

heating the two ends of a bent-round circle of steel. His hands were busy, one on the huge wooden handle of the leather bellows and the other raking coals over the two glowing ends. From the fierce blown coals came a glitter of flying sparks.

"You're dead on time," Ted said, and threw a flick of sand into the flames. The boy saw them turn blue as the sand fell on the steel. "Now git that 'ammer to stand by an' strike. I'll belt it first to make a join."

Continuing words with actions, he hoisted the round steel wheel-rim from the forge onto the anvil. The two glowing ends that had to be joined overlapped, and Ted gave them a clout with his forge hammer. Then another, and another. All his movements were hurried but sure, and the boy saw the ends fuse together.

Ted dusted more sand on the weld and shouted, "Now belt it straight when I tap with me 'ammer. Bring your'n down straight on its face. Don't angle it or you'll dent the metal."

The boy shouted, "Right, Ted. I'm ready," and hefted his seven-pound blacksmith's hammer.

Ted sniffed, then lightly touched a spot on the hot steel with his own tapping hammer. The boy swung. Thump! He felt afraid to strike too hard in case he mis-hit or jarred Ted's hands. He saw himself being chased from the forge by an irate man jumping in agony.

But Ted yelled, "Hit, boy, hit. You ain't dustin' flies off your ears. This steel ain't putty you c'n push with yer fingers."

Ted scuffed his face, wiping the dripping sweat off on

his sleeve. The heat from the forge glared directly on him where he was standing.

The boy swung up his hammer and held his breath in tenseness. This time, after Ted tapped, he brought the hammer down full force. The blow was true, and Ted nodded fleetingly.

"That's it," the boy heard him say. "Now keep it up. It ain't a fairy you're ticklin'."

When at last the two ends glowed, welded securely together, Ted stood them back in the fire. The completed circle of steel was three feet six or more in diameter. As he raked on coals, Ted glanced around slowly at the boy. He was standing doubled over his hammer, gasping for breath.

"Yeah," Ted said. "It takes it out of yer, though a lot of it's knack. Yer don't swing the 'ammer down, just let it fall. Its own weight does the damage."

He pumped the fire to a hot, glowing furnace, readying the steel for its final trim with the tapping hammer. Ted prided himself on doing a first-class welding job. The resulting rim or tire would have a join difficult to see.

The boy sucked a great mouthful of air before he could say, "Yers, but you still got to lift it. An' it's the liftin' that gets yer. I could feel me back tearin' every time I hefted." He shrugged to ease the pain pulling somewhere under his shoulders.

Ted said, "That's all part of growin'. You got to stretch 'em one way or another. Them muscles'll be all the better for it in a day or two. When I've smoothed this orf, we'll go outside to fit it on the wheel."

The boy watched, absorbed again now that his breathing was nearly normal.

"There's a lot to learn," he thought, "every way you look. An' some of it you never can learn. Take ole Ted. He can't ride a horse like Ross an' the others, but look what he's doin' there, workin' that steel."

And suddenly, he wanted to tell Ted what he was thinking. There was a stoop to Ted that reminded the boy of his own loneliness. Perhaps everyone was lonely in their own little way and liked a pat on the back.

"Yers, Ted," the boy said. "I reckon you've done a good job. You wouldn't reckon that steel would join like that. Just goes to show what happens when you know what you're doin'."

He clicked his fingers to Rags to make him come close. The dog had been wary of all the flying sparks.

Ted said, "It's not too bad. Now get a pair of those big tongs." He jerked his thumb toward a tool board on the wall. "No, get two pairs. We'll need two outside when we drop it on the fire."

After a final tap, he threw the hammer down, then sent the steel tire spinning toward the doorway. Each time the still hot weld rolled around, it smoked on the dusty ground. Outside, the wheel tumbled, clanging against some old fencing posts stacked in a heap.

"There yer are," Ted said. "Now all we have to do is fit it."

With the boy and Rags following, he went out into the fierce sun glare. For a moment the impact was blinding after the darkness of the blacksmith's shop, and Ted jerked down his hat brim. The boy screwed his eyelids, unable to raise his hands because of the two heavy tongs.

"We'll try it for a fit first," Ted added, "then set it on

those chips." He nodded toward a ring of wood chips stacked neatly in a circle on the ground. Nearby lay the buggy wheel that had to be fitted.

Working quietly to Ted's quick, short orders, the boy helped him lift the tire onto the wheel, then off again onto the pile of chips. Ted lit them and stepped backward with the boy to watch them blaze. Rags crept under some of the sheltering fenceposts to get away from any more heat.

"We'll let 'er warm," Ted said, "just enough to expand, then slip 'er on. She'll be a good fit by the look of it."

He rubbed his face on a grubby red bandanna, pleased at the way the tire had rested on the wheel. A small amount of expansion would spread it enough to ease it onto the wheel rim. A few taps and a bucket or two of cooling water, and the tire would fit neatly, never to shift.

The fiery circle on the ground licked and spluttered until the steel tire was a smoking blue.

Then Ted shouted, "Now get to 'er quick. You take 'er there, an' I'll take this side. Lift 'er smart an' carry 'er straight. Let 'er down dead on the rim when I tell yer."

The boy felt the fire's heat sear his trousers as he gripped with the tongs, then a further heat coming up to his hands as he and Ted carried the smoking tire. More smoke curled up and stung the boy's eyes when the tire was set on the wooden wheel.

Little tongues of flame flared while Ted shouted, "Git the water an' dribble it on. So help me, don't stand there starin'."

The boy grabbed one of the buckets of water Ted had stood near and dribbled water around the smoldering wheel as Ted tapped the tire into position. At last, when the boy thought he would choke if he swallowed any more steam and smoke, Ted straightened.

"There she is," he said. "All snug an' neat. A coat of paint tomorrow an' she'll be ready for the buggy."

Contentedly, the boy stood aside with Ted and admired the finished job. Though his eyes stung and his back ached, he liked the feeling of having taken part, of having helped.

"If a job's good," he thought, "an' well done, you can't help sort of standin' back an' lookin'. Well, there it is, yer think, and an hour ago there was nothing. Just a strip of steel, an' a wheel with no tire. Now it's right an' finished."

Pleased, as he was at most times with the way he could think things out, he said, "It's a good fit, Ted. Real good. If yer ask me, you couldn't get better."

He bent over the now cool wheel and lightly ran his finger along the join between tire and rim. Barely a ridge rose under his touch.

Ted said, "Yers. Well, that's that. You better nip orf now for something else. I've got a bit of boardin' to repair in the old girl." He slapped the buggy, standing on three wheels with the axle of the fourth one propped on an old oil drum.

The boy walked around the vehicle examining it intently. It reminded him somehow of great, lonely distances and horses pounding along, whisking up dust. He could smell the grease of harness leather on the worn tandem pole.

"I bet she's covered a few miles," he told Ted. "You c'n feel it in the way she's sort of all ribbed an' knotted—as if she's been beltin' along for miles an' miles an' miles."

Ted said, "You'll belt along if Ross comes home an' you're standin' there starin'. An' you'll be ribbed an' knotted, too, if you don't get out of my way. But I know what yer mean," he added, walking with the boy toward the woodheap. "That old buggy could tell a few stories. She's older than the boss, he was tellin' me. His father bought it before he was born."

At the woodheap he left the boy and continued to the toolshed. He wanted some nails and planking that had been specially ordered.

Feeling restless, the boy watched Ted go, then decided to cut some wood. But after a few half-hearted swings with the ax, he drove it into a log.

"Stay there," he said, "an' have a breather. Come on, Rags. We'll see what Roany's doin'."

The sense of pride in ownership was strong in him, and he wished, as he spoke, that the colt could be like Rags—always at his heels.

The urge that drew him to the stables was greater than he could resist. There was a kind of lighthearted scuff in the way his boots clumped, hurrying to the stables.

Rags followed, resigned to the inevitable.

Chapter Four

Lightning

That night a storm rumbled and tossed around Yamboorah homestead, but no rain fell. The boy lay awake listening to the thunder and watching the lightning flare flash through his window. The awful, terrifying claps sometimes made the whole bunkhouse tremble.

"If ole Kanga was here," he thought, sweating in his blankets, "it wouldn't be so bad. I could sort of feel someone was handy if a bolt came whistlin' in. You c'n hear the sizzle of some of that lightnin'."

Glad to have his mind diverted from the storm, he began thinking about Kanga—wondering where he was; what he was doing. He could picture the old dogman sprawled on the ground while the storm raged overhead.

"No wonder he's tough," the boy thought. "Bitter, yer might almost say—though that's the wrong word. His life don't know any softness. Only the hard red ground, an' the weather. Always the weather, tearin' at 'im."

Curled in his blankets, the boy saw the weather as something monstrous. Frightening. Storm, heat, wind, and rain; searing, beating, and smashing; making a man as hard as the raw, bare country; as hard as the gnarled, twisted trees that fought for survival.

"An' that'll be me," he said out loud. "Some day. If I c'n stick it. But I've got this soft bit in me, an' that's the trouble. There ain't no room for softness on a place like Yamboorah."

He was dozing when the lightning struck—a crackling vicious blast that echoed and re-echoed, flashing a blinding light that seemed to rock and sway. The boy felt the air tremble, undulating into his room. Awed, he burrowed deeper into his blankets, then suddenly chilled. Suppose it were the stables! He had heard that horses attracted lightning, especially if they were frightened.

Doubling over, the boy pulled on his boots. Their tightness numbed him, but he ran automatically. Outside, a great column of light flared up torchlike to the sky. In its glow the whole of the Yamboorah buildings stood out clearly. Even the smallest details were outlined sharply.

For a moment the boy stopped, dazzled by the glare. Then his heart steadied. Rags came bounding from the little feed shed. And beyond, the stables stood intact. But the center tree of the row of giant old peppercorns that helped to shelter the homestead was split right down the middle. Its two halves glowed, aflame from the intense heat that had cut them apart.

The boy said, "Cor," and ran on toward the stables.

"First," he thought, "I'll have a look at 'em there an' then come back. I expect the men'll be out to do something."

In the stalls the roan was nibbling anxiously at some hay. Its eyes gleamed, reflecting the outside glow, as it turned to face the boy. In the next two stalls, Powder and Patches nickered softly, more inured than the colt to their confining walls.

"So you're all doin' fine," the boy murmured thankfully. "I guess you're snug at that, though you had me worried. I better git back to see what's happenin'. They might want me t' give a hand." All his words were jerky, choked by the dry, electric air.

As he left, another spear of lightning jagged and ripped at the sky, flooding the stalls with light. It seemed to the boy that the following boom of thunder would flatten the roof down, but he forced himself to run.

"It's no worse than some of the others," he shouted to Rags. "So we won't stay to see. Ross might want us over there at that tree."

Hurdling every shadow that lay in front of him, he raced back past the woodheap. Close to the burning tree, he skidded to a stop. Alici and Maheena, wide-eyed from another frightening sizzle of lightning, were in front of him. Each was loaded with a coil of rope.

"They cut 'im branch," Maheena shouted. "We drag 'im away. Oh dear, oh dear, we frighten too much." She shuddered at the thunder following the lightning's rip.

"Yers," the boy shouted. "I'm a bit scared, too. You can't help it with all this row. Give me one of the ropes an' we'll get started."

He pulled the coil from Maheena's shoulder and ran on. The two girls sprinted, staying close to his side. Rags ran behind, baffled by noise and excitement.

On the two trees at each side of the burning one, groups

of men were clustered, lopping the branches. Without being told, the boy knew what was being done.

"They're loppin' 'em," he thought, "so that they don't
catch an' set the lot of 'em goin'. If that happened, we'd
have a real big fire that no one could stop."

Ross was at the base of one tree, shouting instructions;
the boss was at the other, doing the same. A glitter
of sparks dripped like a shower of gold from the burning
trunk. And as a limb fell, hacked from one of the neighboring trees, the shower puffed up and outward.

"Get 'em away," the boss shouted when he saw the boy
and girls. "An' don't waste time. Get 'em clear of the sparks
as quick as you can."

Glancing up again, he anxiously peered through the
leafy branches at two men climbing to reach the top.

"Careful," he continued shouting. "An' watch how you
go. Don't drop a branch on Joe down below. He's halfway
through that big 'un." His shout ended as he jumped aside
to dodge a falling bough.

The boy looped his rope around a limb and began to
haul. Somewhere, he knew, Alici and Maheena were doing
the same. As his boots dug into the sandy soil, he felt the
weight of the pull ease and glanced over his shoulder. Mrs.
Jones was there, dressed in a pair of the boss's trousers and
one of his shirts.

She was straining on the rope as much as he was, and
he had a sudden memory.

"Cor!" he shouted. "It's just like when yer bunked me
up to the kitchen chimney. You remember? In that dust
storm." The rope bit into his shoulder, and he took a fresh
grip.

"Yes," Mrs. Jones called back. "I remember. Now save your breath for pulling. I want all mine if you don't."

The boy thought she chuckled, though he wasn't sure.

"She's funny," he thought, and bent over almost doubled with the strain. "You never c'n tell. Sometimes she's worried when you think she's laughin', an' cryin', when you think she ought t' be glad. I s'pose she's nervy, one way or another."

To make sure that she didn't have to pull too hard, he hauled until he wondered whether she were still behind him. Looking around, he saw that she was. Her head was bent, bowed on a body that was unused to such work. As Ross had once said, "She's a good 'un if ever there was one."

Near the woodheap, the boy shouted, "We'll leave it here, Mrs. Jones. I'll bring the rope back."

Mrs. Jones said, "All right, I'll help Alici and Maheena. If we all work together, we can move them all the quicker." And she hurried to where the two girls were struggling with an enormous bough. The two were as surprised to see her as the boy had been.

"By cri', Missus Jones," Alici gasped to say, "you more better in bed. Dis work no good for anyone got 'im soft hands."

But both girls were glad of Mrs. Jones's help. The weight of the bough had been almost too much for them.

Back again in the shower of glittering sparks, the boy hitched his rope to another bough. So, too, did Alici and Maheena, while Mrs. Jones again helped the boy, then gave a final tug or two to aid the girls.

And gradually the dry, fierce storm passed, leaving only

the blazing trunk to give light. In its fading, crumbling glare, the men came down from lopping the neighboring limbs and finished hauling them away.

Mrs. Jones made tea in the kitchen, and the boy helped Alici and Maheena carry big, steaming billyfuls to where the men stood around the now softly glowing trunk. The boss was standing to one side talking to Ross when the boy handed them both a mug of hot tea.

"We stopped it from spreading," the boy heard the boss say, "but that's about all. I was proud of this row of trees, an' now there'll be a gap. Never grow another one, not in my lifetime."

He drank from the mug, and there was a kind of sadness in the way he wiped his hand over his mouth afterward—as if he were brushing away the years and the things he knew he could not accomplish.

"Yers," Ross agreed. "It takes a long time. A tree's got something—especially these big old fellers—that nothing else has. You see 'em standin' there, an' nothing seems to touch 'em. Wind, rain, storm. Then, zip. You get one like this"—he waved with his hand toward the smoldering stump—"an' it hurts yer deep inside. Like seein' an' old mate go."

Burly on his straddled stockman's legs, he drained his mug in one great gulp, then tossed it to the boy. Striding away, he began gathering the axes and ropes that had been used and checked them carefully. Ross was a man who gave attention to every detail.

Later, sitting on the woodheap with Alici and Maheena and drinking the remaining tea, the boy said, "So there you are. The storm's gone, an' the tree's burnt. All them years for nothing, you might say."

And suddenly he stopped, flooded by a worrying thought. "What about the galahs?" he whispered. "There must've been hundreds of 'em roosting in that tree." He stared through the hushed, breathless darkness, now that all the men were gone.

Alici shivered and cupped her mug in her hands. Maheena drew up her knees until her dress spread around her in the shape of a tent.

"Yers," she whispered, peering toward the stump. "Galah fella burn, every one. But tomorrow"—she lifted her arms, fluttering them gently—"other fella come, fly all the same dis." She waved her hands almost invisibly in the darkness, and the boy watched her, fascinated. "They come from other tree, other place, an' they all the same. S'pose one die, he no die finis'." She stared at the boy, luminous-eyed from the glowing stump's reflection.

The boy hunched stiffly. "Yeah," he said at last. "I see what you mean. Or think I do. One galah is like another, like you an' me are like other people. Suppose one dies, it don't really matter—there's always someone comin' along to fill the place."

Alici drew up *her* knees and billowed out her dress the same as Maheena's.

"True," she whispered. "True too much. You savvy 'im other day we see blackfella's tracks for corroboree. Das why they make 'im. Egg all the same new life. Dey hold 'im up to hot dry sky."

She cupped her hands again as she had around the mug,

though this time they were empty, holding an imaginary egg.

"Den rain smell 'im egg. Hear 'im li'le life cheep inside. Den rain come tumblin' down. You savvy, by 'n by?"

The boy nodded. He could see the egg she held and the slim black hands outlined in darkness.

"Yers," he said. "Now I'm gettin' it clear. You mean that the storm tonight an' the corroboree are all sort of tied in together. The dead galahs, too, are part of it. When the rain comes, there'll be new grass, new life, an' new everything you might say."

He paused for a moment, baffled for words in what he was trying to express, before he added, "Makes yer sad, though, when yer think of the things that have to happen. Like them galahs dyin', burnt to death."

Maheena said, "We sad, too. Maybe some 'nother time we talk a li'le more. Now s'pose we go sleep, Missus Jones or boss come lookin'. They cross s'pose we no go."

"Yes," the boy said, and stood up to gather the mugs and billies. "You're right. I've got a fair ole day ahead of me tomorrow, tidyin' up some of these boughs. There'll be a good stack of logs to dry by the time I finish."

The boughs, when cut, would have to drain their sap and season in the sun before they could be used for burning.

The two girls nodded and left, creeping quietly on their bare calloused feet. The boy followed, loaded with the empty mugs and billies.

At the garden gate, he called, "Good night," to the girls and told Rags to, "Sit down, mate. I'll see you later."

In the kitchen he dumped the utensils in the sink and rinsed them under the tap.

"They'll be right," he thought, "for Mrs. Jones in the morning. One way an' another, she's had a pretty busy day an' a fair ole scare. That thunder an' lightning nearly tore the roof off."

After drying the mugs and billies, he set them in their places, then went outside again.

Trudging past the gate, he called, "Good night, Rags. You better nip off to the shed till mornin'. I'll see you then, when I'm havin' a go at that wood."

Boy and dog parted, each to his separate ways, and on his bunk the boy thought over all that had happened. The storm, the tree, Ross and the boss talking, and Alici and Maheena, as well as Mrs. Jones hauling on the rope.

"It's great," he said, and closed his eyes, "the way they're all sort of close around yer. Not sayin' much, but just enough to show they're with yer. An' her pullin' that rope was more than anyone expected."

His last thoughts were of the stump glowing bright in the darkness.

As Ross had said, "It hurts yer deep to see an old mate go."

He wondered whether the tree could feel the agony of its passing.

Chapter Five

"Go Walkabout"

When the boy awoke, dawn was a smudged raw haze. As he stamped his boots after pulling them on, he felt the heat already pulsing in through the window.

"Phew!" he thought. "That storm made little difference. An' I reckon first I'll take a close look at that stump. Might still be burnin', but I doubt it."

His hands moved swiftly, tucking in his shirt. He liked to feel it buckled in snugly to his waist.

Outside, the warm, tangy air had the taint of smoke. There was a hazy drift, too, that had hung all night around the homestead. It was wisped into ghostly vaporings that made the boy stare. It seemed to him he was hurrying through a huge gray cobweb that broke to his touch, then closed in behind him again.

And as he imagined himself floating through the mist, caught up in the dawn's quiet eeriness, he saw the stump. It stood up straight in two black halves, halfway along the row of giant old peppercorn trees. The trunk was solid for a few feet up, then split apart.

"Like a tooth," the boy said, walking toward it, "that's gone bad. No wonder the boss felt sad about it."

He walked around in the ash, scuffing his boots. In the neighboring trees, lopped one-sidedly, galahs were already gathering. Their rosy-breasted forms bobbed and chattered.

"So there you are," the boy told them, looking up. "You c'n reckon yourselves lucky. There was a few of yer mates on this ole tree that you'll never see again. An' I c'n tell you this much." He paused to give emphasis. "It could have been worse. The lot could've burned, an' you with 'em, if we hadn't worked to save yer." Pleased with the way he had explained things, he turned away.

The galahs bunched, peering down. As the boy had said, they would have died but for the firefighters, for birds on a bough, like fowls on a perch, seem almost incapable of movement after they have roosted. And had the birds flown, the blinding sheets of flame would have drawn them back into the holocaust.

Beyond the little feed shed, a stockman was riding from the horse yards to muster the horses. As he cantered, barely seen in the mist, Rags came from the shed and stretched. He saw the boy and came full tilt toward him, belly flat to the ground. Close to the woodheap now, the boy caught the dog and rolled him over. Covered in dust and wood chips, Rags leaped back to squat at the boy's feet.

"That's it," the boy said. "Nice an' steady like. We don't want you growin' into one of these half-witted sort that yap all over a feller. Ole Kanga would never forgive me."

With Rags settled near, the boy began to chop wood. From the kitchen chimney, a thin trail of smoke curled dark against the sky. He guessed Mrs. Jones was busy at the stove.

"By the time this barrer's full," the boy told Rags, "the tea'll be made, an' I'll be right for a mug. But I c'n tell yer this: I'll bet she's tired. An' the two girls, too. It was a rough old night, whichever way you look at it."

When the barrow was full, he wheeled it to the kitchen. Inside, Mrs. Jones stood neat and smiling, though he thought her eyes looked tired.

"Hello," she said, and put some steak into pans. "I heard you chopping while I lit the fire. You could have slept late, you know, and nobody would have bothered. Alici and Maheena haven't come out yet." She turned a steak with a long steel fork.

The boy said, "Aw, I dunno, Mrs. Jones. I like it real early. It's kind of clean, without any fuss. No one's around to see what you do or where you go. Not," he went on, dumping down an armful of wood, "that they do. I mean, come round lookin' to see what I'm doin'." He paused again, tied, as he often was, for words. "Yer know what I mean, though I can't quite say it. The dawn's got something you never can." From force of habit, he sat on the woodbox, waiting for a mug of tea.

Mrs. Jones handed him one, then said, "Yes, I know what you mean. Sometimes I stand outside to catch the first breath. It's lovely to feel the untouched freshness."

The boy liked her words and sat there quietly drinking. From the distances beyond the surroundings, he could hear the drum of hoofbeats. The stockman's whip echoed and re-echoed, beating against the quiet.

"Yes," the boy thought. "She's got it there. Feelin' the

untouched freshness. Funny how people can say just the right thing." And he remembered Ross talking about the burning tree.

Later, with Rags at his heels, he fed the stabled horses and stopped to talk to Roany.

"You came through well," he said, patting the glossy neck. "Through all that row an' clatter. I'll bet there were times when you wondered what was happenin'. It's different for yer, shut in a stable. I reckon, out in the scrub, horses get more or less used to it."

The colt nickered, and after a time the boy left contentedly. He could hear Ross outside, talking with the men. They were stalking in and out of the saddle room, fetching their saddles and bridles. The whinny of horses milling in the horse yards meant that the day was really starting.

Perched high on a horse-yards post, the boy watched the men saddle and leave. Ross rode in the lead, balanced lightly on his horse.

"He's more at home in a saddle," the boy said, sliding down to the ground, "than he is on his feet. Yer wouldn't think such a big man could sit so easy. He don't move when the horse shies or capers."

As the cavalcade, led by Ross, swung to pass the wood-heap, an aboriginal had trouble with his mount. It reared high, then came down bucking, nearly unseating its rider. Horse and man rocked and swayed, pitched into a jumbled, squealing frenzy.

"Stick 'im, Wirra," the boy shouted, running closer. "Stay with 'im if yer can. He's nearly got 'is feet through the bridle."

But Wirranoona grunted, "Me got 'im true," and finally reined the horse's head up.

With a yell that scared the galahs from the trees, the aboriginal spurred the horse forward. As one, the cavalcade went with it, splattering up dust in a wild, headlong gallop. Ross held the lead, eager—as the men were—to race for a few hundred yards. Afterward, the boy knew, they would settle the horses down to their usual jog-trotting pace.

Watching excitedly, the boy clambered onto a mound of logs stacked on the woodheap. Rags followed, puzzled, but sensing the excitement.

"Go on!" the boy shouted. "Go on, Joe! Go on, Charlie! See if yer c'n beat ole Ross in the lead!"

But Ross drew away and soon outdistanced all the others, then held up his hand. The stockmen reined in their horses, haunching them down suddenly to a quick, prancing walk behind the overseer.

"That's it," the boy told Rags, and scrambled from the woodpile. "Old Ross says woa, an' they do it. That's the end, he tells 'em, of our bit of fun; now finish. We got work t' do, remember!"

Pleased at the way he had guessed at what Ross was saying, the boy began to chop. His hands felt the worn, smooth ax handle slide in his grasp. He liked the feel of the rhythmic rise and fall as the blade bit in and out of wood.

"It's like something yer know," he thought. "Where yer don't have to think. You see the log, an' yet yer really don't. Yer got other things to think while the ole ax belts away."

The heap of chopped wood was as high as his knees when Alici came through the garden gateway. She was swinging a snake around and around by its tail, and the boy glanced up, horrified. His ax almost chopped into his foot before he deflected it.

"Hey," he tried to shout, his voice croaked. "What d'yer think you're doin'? That wriggler's still alive, an' deadly. Look at 'is jaws mouthin' away at yer!"

Alici kept the snake whirling while she watched it carefully. Sweat from the heat beaded her face. Otherwise, she seemed unconcerned. Each time the snake tried to coil, she gave it an extra flick that made it straighten.

Close to the boy, she said, "This one 'e bad too much. Me see 'im tail poke out from under woodbox, so grab 'im take 'im come. S'pose by 'n by you no see 'im. You put 'im wood along woodbox. Zip, 'e bite 'im you quick time."

The boy guessed she meant the outside woodbox, where he kept an emergency supply. It was an upended old galvanized iron tank, stood against the kitchen wall.

"Yeah," he managed to say, mesmerized by the whirling snake. "But what about you? Bang 'is head quick, an' I'll finish 'im with this ax." He warily lifted the ax and braced himself to bring it down.

Alici shook her head. "No," she said. "Me crack dis one, all the same whip. You watch 'im. 'Is head fly off, quick time."

With a sudden deft swing, she cracked the snake, and its head severed cleanly, flying past the boy.

"Cor," he said, ducking instinctively. "That's a neat way of doin' 'em. I'll bet it took yer a long time to learn. The first one," he added, "must've had yer scared. Sort of worried whether you could do it." He stared at Alici, wanting to pat her but rubbing his own head instead.

Alici said, "No. Mother, Father belong me savvy for do

it plenty time. They show me"—her white teeth gleamed as she suddenly smiled shyly—"when me li'le piccanin all der same dis." She lowered the snake's body until her hand was two feet from the ground. "You savvy? All der same dis."

"Yeah," the boy agreed. "I savvy. An' no wonder you're good. I wouldn't do it, not if I was treadin' on one."

He ran across to shoo Rags away from the snake's head, which glinted evilly in the sun. With a few quick scrapes of his boot heel, the boy dug a hole in the dust and wood chips, then kicked the head into it.

"That'll stop you," he told Rags, "from takin' any chances. You never know. You might take a chew of poison or something."

When he jogged back to Alici, she said, "No, you never must. Grab 'im snake, I mean. You an' me not the same two fella." She held up two fingers. "You one dis place." She scratched a line in the dust with her toe, between her feet and the boy's. "Me dis place. We walk along together, but no all the same." Her face wrinkled in concentration while she spoke, trying to state her thoughts clearly.

The boy nodded. There was a kind of remonstrance in Alici's soft, guttural voice that he liked hearing—as if she were older and knew far more than he would ever know. He wished they could sit on a log and continue talking, but she still held the snake's body in her hands.

"Yeah," he said. "I know what you mean. Yet we get along fine. I reckon you an' me an' Maheena have some pretty good times. Though now we're at it, what about the snake? I'll bury 'im if yer like, somewhere around here." He gestured around at the ground and the scattered woodpile.

Alici said, "No. By 'n by tonight, me an' Maheena eat 'im. Put 'im in ash for bake. He plenty good too much." She rubbed her stomach, spreading her long fingers gently.

The boy scratched his head, puzzled for what to say. "If I pull a face," he thought, "or screw up me nose, she'll think I'm funny. They eat 'em, an' that's all there is to it."

Aloud, he said, "Aw, well, if that's what you're gonna do, I wouldn't let Mrs. Jones see yer. She'd reckon you got enough t' eat without eatin' snakes."

Mention of Mrs. Jones reminded him the morning was passing. There were a few more jobs to do yet before dinnertime.

Alici twirled the snake into a loop of coils, then tucked them against her side. As she covered them over with part of her loose dress, the boy noticed the coils were still squirming.

"You want to watch out," he said, "or you'll lose 'im. If yer like, I'll nip into me room an' get you a sugar bag. There's one pushed under me pillow."

But Alici was confident. Her white, clean teeth flashed again for a moment.

"No lose 'im," she said, and left the boy suddenly.

He noticed the sway of her dress as she clutched the snake to her. Then he realized why she was hurrying. The boss was at the garden gate, just pushing it open. As he came on, he stared after Alici. By the time she reached the fence by the big watering trough and climbed through, the boss stopped close to the boy. Both stared at each other solemnly; then the boss raised his eyebrows.

"Where's she off to?" he asked. "An' what's got into

you? She's supposed to be in the kitchen or makin' the beds or something."

The boy said, "Yeah, that's what she was doin'. She came out to tell me what was wanted, then . . . then . . ." He screwed his eyes for a moment. "Then went on round there t' get some mint. She's goin' in through the back way to the garden." He finished in a hurry, pleased he had thought of an excuse.

The boss said, "*Mint!* There's not a leaf in the garden. An' there won't be until we get some rain. But never mind. I'll see to her later. The thing is now, have yer seen Ted around?"

"Yeah," the boy said. "He's over paintin' the buggy. I saw 'im mixin' paint. I'll get him if yer like."

The remembrance came of Ted bent over a paint pot and the newly tired wheel now fitted to the buggy. The vehicle stood, when fully painted, ready and waiting for whatever the boss might order.

The boss rubbed his chin and said, "No. I'll see 'im myself," and continued on past the woodheap.

Rags was sniffing near the buried head, though the boy beckoned quietly with his fingers. The boss seemed not to notice; yet his back had a knowing kind of awareness.

"He don't say much," the boy muttered, "but them eyes of 'is see the lot. He just sort of looks right on past yer, but they're nippin' about takin' notice of everything."

And skirting around the little feed shed, the boss glanced back over his shoulder.

"They get on fine," he thought. "But reckon they're more or less mysterious. The trouble is, they ain't. It stands out a mile they were up to something. If I miss my guess, that girl had 'er hand tucked in her dress, an' the dog knew a thing or two. Between 'em, I reckon a snake comes into it. Alici dug in her toes when she dragged that one from under the woodbox."

He continued on his way, chuckling. His life had been spent, almost as much as an aboriginal's, in reading signs on the ground. He had seen the tracks Alici made near the woodbox.

In the kitchen Mrs. Jones had her problems. She wanted Alici to help prepare dinner and couldn't find her anywhere. Exasperated, she called for Maheena to come and help. Both were busy when the boy trundled his wheelbarrow to a halt outside.

"Here we are, Mrs. Jones," he said, coming in with an armful of wood. "This ought t' be enough to see you through for the day. I've cut some small stuff to give you real heat."

As he dumped the wood down into the woodbox, he stared hopefully at the teapot. He thought he could see a faint wisp of steam drifting from the spout.

Mrs. Jones said, "Yes, go ahead and pour a cup for yourself. There's some buttered scones still on the sideboard. Have you seen Alici? She slipped out for a moment, and I haven't seen her since. I've never known her to do it before."

Unlike the boss, Mrs. Jones saw everything as she planned it, neat and orderly, with a set routine. Yet at times she coped tremendously against what seemed insurmountable odds.

The boy thought quickly while he poured out tea. The pot was hot, and he felt it burn his knuckles.

"If she's anywhere," he thought, "she's out there near her room, hangin' up that snake or peelin' it."

For a moment he had the fear she might have been bitten, but shrugged this away when he said, "No." Then added, "Yeah, she came round by the woodheap. The last I saw of her she was comin' in again. D'yer want me to go an' find her?" He pronounced his aitches, hoping to please Mrs. Jones.

She said, "Yes, if you would. But drink your tea first. Maheena and I are all right for the present."

She smiled at Maheena, and the girl nodded her dark, eager head. She was immaculate, but the heat in the kitchen made her young face shine with sweat.

"Yers," Maheena nodded to say. "By 'n' by me cross too much with Alici. She bad for not comin' back."

The boy sipped his tea. He could sense that Mrs. Jones was nervy by the way she moved her hands.

"Aw, I dunno," he said slowly. "You never know how it is. She might've tore her dress or something, gettin' through the fence."

As he spoke, he could see Alici struggling through the wires with the snake clutched to her.

"She's in a lot of trouble," was the thought in his mind, "all over a bloomin' snake. I wonder what's got into her, t' make her do it."

Mrs. Jones glanced up in surprise. "A fence?" she asked. "What fence? She uses the gate like everyone else, doesn't she?"

The boy said, "Yes! But you know. I was just sort of sayin'," and decided to leave.

"If I stay here," he thought, "they'll go round an' round,

an' then—there you are. They'll have me trapped, an' I'll have to tell 'em."

Gulping his tea in one great scalding mouthful, he added, "I'll see where she is. More 'n likely she's comin' now, trampin' along the path."

He pushed outside quickly, letting the wire gauze door ease shut behind him. Going on past the big, sprawling homestead, he stared around quickly. He knew the room she shared with Maheena was somewhere beyond the block of stockmen's quarters and hoped to find it by some kind of sign—a dress hanging on a line outside or perhaps seeing Alici through an open window.

He noticed a room with bright, fluttery curtains that reminded him of the girls' dresses. They dressed alike, under Mrs. Jones's supervision, and he was sure he had seen the colored patterns before.

"That's them," he said, walking close to a window. "You c'n sort of see it flutterin' round their legs. Hey, there, Alici!" he added in a shout. "Mrs. Jones wants yer. She's goin' round in circles, worryin'."

But no answering call came from inside. The boy banged the wall, then scratched his head.

"Well, well, well," he said. "She ain't there. Now where do I look?"

Walking away from the window, he saw some tracks in the dust that could have been Alici's or Maheena's. He knew that Alici had a twisted little toe, but his skill wasn't good enough to read that in the dust.

"If I was Ross, or one of 'em," he muttered wishfully, "I could read 'em easy. But I ain't, so there we are."

He followed the tracks swiftly, peering down at the ground. The imprints were easy to see, splayed in the red, powdery dust.

After climbing out through the rear fence that bounded Yamboorah homestead and stockmen's buildings, the boy found Alici sitting on a log. She still had the snake with her and was staring disconsolately back the way she had come. She saw the boy long before he saw her. As he walked up to her, she turned away to hide her face.

The boy said, "I been lookin' everywhere. Mrs. Jones says she's gettin' dinner, an' you ought t' be there to help 'er."

He kicked his boot toe hard, stubbing it in the dust. Alici seemed to have changed since he had last spoken to her. The rigid set of her shoulders had an air about them that worried him, as if she had changed suddenly into someone he could not understand.

Alici shrugged stiffly. "Me finis' along dis place," she whispered, more to herself than the boy. "Me go walk-about, you savvy? Go walkabout 'long Bush for see 'im everything, you understand?" Her voice quickened, sounding louder as it rose.

The boy felt his chin sag. "So that's what's got into 'er," he thought. "I thought she was funny before, jumpin' around with that snake."

Aloud, he said, "Walkabout? You can't do that. What about Maheena an' Mrs. Jones? The two of 'em's there, waitin' for yer. The boss, too 'll have a thing or two to say."

Alici shrugged again and said, "Tell 'im me see the big rain come. Smell the green, new grass. An' watch 'im the piccanin emu break from its shell. Then run where the ibis

cry, flyin' against the sky." She held out her arms, dangling
the snake.

The boy felt baffled, puzzled for what to say or
do. Something, he knew, was surging strongly in the girl,
and he also knew the same thing happened in aboriginal
men. But Alici and Maheena had always seemed somehow different from other aborigines.

At last he said, "If that's what the drought is doin' to
yer, I'm sorry. But we all have a job to do. You can't go on
walkin' an' walkin' until you're clean over the skyline." A
further thought made him add, "Unless you're a swagman
or something." Carried on by his words, he began to
trudge around the log, waving his hands at Alici.

She watched him furtively from under lowered eyelids.

The boy sensed her gaze and stopped suddenly, to jab a finger toward her.

"Now look," he went on. "You an' Maheena are always sort of tellin' me; now I'm tellin' you." He wagged the finger, then rammed his hands in his pockets. "You come on back an' forget all this." He pulled out a hand again to wave around at the vast, silent Bush. "An' you'll be glad. Throw that ole snake away, too. You don't want it there, danglin' in your hands. An' as for your walkabout feelin', do what I do—get an ax or something an' belt away at some wood."

He chuckled, imagining Alici chopping on the woodheap.

Alici said, "So you savvy? You sometime got 'im this fella who want to go walkabout inside you?" She looked up at the boy appealingly, widening her eyes, so that he could look directly at them.

"Sure," the boy said. "We all have. Look at Mrs. Jones. She was goin' to leave some time ago. I tried to, when I ran away. You come on back an' have some dinner. After that, you'll forget all about it."

He took the snake from her unresisting hand and flung it away, then awkwardly touched her arm.

"Come on," he added. "That wriggler caused most of the trouble. Catchin' him like yer did sort of stirred you up, made you in a way want to do what some of the other abos do."

"Yers," Alici said, beginning to walk with the boy. "Maybe true. Maybe true too much. Maybe by 'n by dis fella stop." She touched her chest. "He no tell 'im leg for go walkabout."

"That's it," the boy told her. "He won't say a word, nor me either. You see! This afternoon you'll be skippin' around doin' the washing-up, an' you won't hear a whisper. Just me an' Mrs. Jones, or maybe Maheena, tellin' yer a yarn. Come on quick, before they ring that dinner bell."

He left Alici outside her room and walked on to the kitchen. Mrs. Jones was there with Maheena, getting ready to ring the bell. They both looked around expectantly when the boy pushed open the door.

"Yeah," he said, in answer to their unasked question. "I found her all right. She was feelin' a bit crook, but she's on her way now. Be here in a minute."

And to his surprise neither Mrs. Jones nor Maheena said anything. Instead, Mrs. Jones served his dinner, and Maheena rang the bell, jangling it loudly.

"So what can you make of that?" the boy thought, and ravenously ate his dinner. "They must have been talkin' or known all along. You c'n never tell what some of 'em are thinking."

Then he chewed contentedly, watching Alici come in through the doorway. Maybe they had wanted him to find her and do a bit of reasoning. He saw Mrs. Jones's quick smile when she handed him another helping.

Chapter Six

Breaking a Colt

"When you're through," Ross told the boy a few mornings later, "give Joe a hand. He's puttin' a couple of nags in the buggy. One of 'em's never been in before, an' he might give some trouble."

Ross was standing near the woodheap, rolling a cigarette. His glance was following a group of stockmen catching and saddling horses at the horse yards. He could see Joe slipping a halter onto a young, rearing colt.

The boy stared, too. There was sleek, flowing youth in the way the colt was rearing.

"Like fire," the boy thought, "lickin' an' burnin' that stump. R'arin' up, then dyin' down before another lick. That feller's full of steam if ever I saw one."

Aloud, he said, "Yeah, I'd like to. Will he call, or shall I go over?"

Head-bent again, he began to swing his ax. A stack of wood lay already cut near the barrow.

Ross said, "He'll call when he's ready. The main thing is to do what he says an' don't go gettin' kicked. An' another thing," he added before heading for the horse yards.

"Don't tell Mrs. Jones. Say you're sort of messin' about or something if she asks you. You know how she is about —well"—he shrugged his shoulders—"yer know, an' I don't have to tell yer."

"Yeah," the boy said. "I know. She won't hear a whisper. You c'n take it from me."

He spoke jerkily, between swings of his ax, then straightened to wipe his face. Heat from the rising sun seemed to burn right through him as he leaned on his ax.

"How long," he went on to ask, "do yer reckon this'll last? The heat, I mean. That lightnin' eased it a bit, but it's worse th'n ever now."

Ross said, "Till it rains. An' the signs are it won't be long. Well! Keep yer ears open for sound of Joe when he calls."

Still with his gaze fixed on the horse yards, Ross began to stride toward them. His back had a stiff, square set to it that the boy often envied—as if he would march straight at anything in front of him, whether it was animal, element, or human.

The boy stood for a moment, watching him go.

"The same ole Ross," he told Rags. "An' the same ole ways. Set, yer might say, t' face what he's got to. Heat, sun, dust, or rain, he don't care either way so long as there's a job he knows wants doin'."

Rags sniffed and stretched out yawning, while the boy went on chopping. Some crows on the killing pens cawed bleakly at the barrenness around them. Even the big old peppercorn trees were growing grayer in their leaves.

"It can't last," the boy thought, chopping slowly. "There must come a time when it's cool an' the rain fallin'. Fallin' an' fallin' until everything's soaked an' sodden. Cor, it'd be great to see something green."

With the thought still wistfully in his mind, he wheeled wood to the kitchen before searching for eggs.

Under the wide saltbush hedge, he felt cooler. The sun couldn't penetrate, though the dust was warm as he crawled. Deciding to have a few minutes free from the fierce, glaring sun, he rolled onto his back. The thick, tangled branches above his face made him think of veins.

"Some's straight, some's crooked," he thought. "Like those on me hand an' arm. An' come to think of it, that's what they are—all of 'em suckin' in something to keep the ole bush goin'."

Soon the hens grew used to him lying there and began to scratch near his head. A big, shaggy-feathered rooster spread his wings to crow defiance.

"Hold on," the boy said, and chuckled. "I'm not doin' anything. Just sort of takin' things in while I have a spell."

He was counting the twigs on a branch when a bellow from the horse yards startled him.

"That's Joe," he muttered, and rolled over again to his stomach.

With the half-full billy of eggs in his hand, he began to edge backward. Another bellow from Joe made him scurry faster.

Once on his feet, he shouted, "O.K., Joe, I'll be with yer," and ran around to the kitchen.

Mrs. Jones asked, as she took the eggs, "Who was that shouting?"

Her face was flushed, as it nearly always was, from the heat both in and outside the kitchen. Permanent rings of damp clung around the lids of her eyes.

"Aw, that was Joe," the boy told her, wanting to stay for his usual mug of tea. But a further roar from Joe set him running again.

In the horse yards, Joe had two horses harnessed. One was the colt the boy had seen earlier. It now stood fidgeting uneasily at the strange feel of harness. An angry, swirling hiss came from the swish of its tail.

The boy steadied to approach slowly as the colt bucked, and Joe led it away from the fence.

Clinging to the lead clipped to the bridle rings, Joe shouted, "You bring the other one. You c'n hook 'im up while I hang on to this feller."

He let the colt kick and buck while he was shouting, and added over his shoulder, "It'll do 'im good to let off steam—be less trouble to get him started."

The boy said, "Whew! He looks pretty frisky to me," and unhitched the other horse to lead it to the buggy.

After strapping its collar to the pole, he walked around carefully to hook the traces onto the swinglebar.

"He's in," he told Joe quietly. "Now what do I do?"

In a sudden, swift picture that flashed through his mind, he saw himself being kicked—felt his body lying battered and bruised under the buggy.

But Joe's slow voice drawled, "Nothin'! Just stand by that old feller while I put this one in."

The boy did as Joe had said, and Joe edged the colt close to the buggy pole. Then he tied a cloth over the animal's eyes before he buckled both horses together at their bit rings with tandem driving reins.

Working with quiet, sure hands, Joe strapped the colt's collar to the pole and eased along its flanks to hook the traces. Finally, he gathered the reins in one hand before climbing up to the high seat.

"When I'm set," he told the boy, "pull the cloth orf the young 'un an' climb up quickly. If he moves too fast, come up the back way."

The boy said, "Sure," and waited.

He watched Joe settle with his feet braced and the reins gripped firmly in both hands; then taking a great breath, he whipped off the cloth.

For a paused, fractional moment, colt, boy, and partnering horse were still. A hush of waiting seemed to lock everything into unmoving quietness. And even before he jumped, the boy knew the colt was moving faster. Its forehoofs swished past his shirt in a cavorting rear that almost trampled him.

Then, buffeted by the colt's shoulder, the boy rolled over and over sideways as the buggy whirled around him in fast, jerking motion. The colt was doubled in a series of fast, twisting bucks that scared him. Yet Joe was untroubled.

Braced firmly on the seat, Joe grinned as the boy scrambled upright. "Come on," he shouted, "an' make it snappy. You ain't got all day to stand there dreamin'."

The boy nodded and started to run. Striding full stretch after the buggy, he caught the back seat in a flying grip that lifted him from his feet. Pulled swiftly, he doubled his knees and landed on the buggy behind Joe.

The boy gasped to get his breath as he shouted, "I'm here, Joe. Yer don't have to worry. I caught it on the way past."

He climbed over the back of the rocking, swaying seat to sit beside Joe. The two bumped together before the boy could get settled.

"Worry?" Joe said. "Who's worryin'? Keep yer legs braced an' a good grip with yer hands. Whatever you do, don't fall orf."

Gripped in his hands, the reins stretched tight with strain. Both horses were galloping now, jaws clamped on their bits. The colt alternately tried to kick or buck, but the speed of the other horse dragged it on.

Watching Joe drive, the boy thought, "That's how he

does it. Lets the quiet one race to keep the other one
movin'. If he was to stop, he'd kick the buggy to pieces—
us, too, I reckon, because we ain't all that far from 'em."

His glance, as he rocked, was fixed on the two pounding rumps beneath him. They rose and fell in a great, driving rhythm that was frightening yet powered with excitement.

"It's because they're alive," he whispered, forgetting Joe
was near. "You can't switch 'em off like a car, but have to
humor 'em. Get 'em to come your way just by the feel of
the reins."

Joe laughed and shouted a great whoop at the horses
before he glanced at the boy. By now the giant old peppercorn trees were passed, and the buggy was bouncing freely
over rough, dusty ground.

"You've got it there," Joe bawled in the boy's ear. "So
help me, you have. Humor 'em, an' get the feel of the reins.
Boy, oh boy, that's the best yet."

Caught in his own wild, rowdy exuberance or the drumming thud of the horses, he began to sing—not loudly, but
more to himself than to the boy or the galloping, straining
animals.

Yet the boy strained to listen. He liked to hear any of
the stockmen sing their sad, lonely songs. Joe, in particu-
lar, had a deep, chesty voice that could rumble right down
inside him.

When Joe reached a song that the boy knew, he joined
in. Rocking and swaying exaggeratedly to the headlong
speed of the horses, they sang together, with Joe adding occasional yodels of harmony.

Finally, having sung all the songs he knew, Joe spat

dryly. "Now," he said, "we'll get down to business. The young 'un's had a fair run, so we'll steady 'im. If he kicks, you hop over into the back seat. They've got a habit, sometimes, of puttin' their feet in yer lap."

The boy said, "I'm right. I'll be watchin'."

Since the singing, he felt closer somehow to Joe, as if he had grown up quickly to be near Joe's ease and strength. His own hands itched to reach for the tight, straining leather.

"Me an' Joe," he thought, exhilarated and happy, "singin' away t'gether an' laughin'. Rippin' along in a buggy. Yer wouldn't believe it if yer didn't know it was true. Feel the ole seat bouncin' under yer trousers."

Eagerly, he watched Joe use the reins, working on the horses' mouths. Steadying them, too, with his coaxing, soothing voice. The boy almost stopped breathing when the colt broke to a fast, unaccustomed trot, and the other horse did likewise.

"You've got 'em, Joe," he said. "They're as right as rain. The colt ain't even humpin'."

Joe said, "Yeah, he's not too bad. I'll swing 'em soon an' head for home. In two or three days he'll make a decent harness horse."

There was pleasure and pride in Joe's voice as he spoke. He loved horses, without any sentimental emotion. They were part of the life that endured the vast, barren landscape. Without them he would have felt useless. Lonely, too, even among friends, even with the boy sitting quietly beside him. They were as essential as the hands with which he touched them.

The boy sensed what Joe was thinking. "Yer love 'em,

Joe, don't yer?" he said. "Horses, I mean. You c'n see it
when you give 'em a rub. Not like me when I'm makin' a
fuss of Roany, but a sort of . . . aw, I dunno, but yer
know what I mean." He ended lamely, trailing the words
into a mumble.

Joe said, "Yeah, I know what yer mean. But don't get
cryin' yer eyes out. The' ain't one of 'em wouldn't kick
your brains out if yer had any. And," he added emphatically, "a man who works with 'em hasn't, take it from me."
He twitched the reins, gently slapping them down on the
horses' rumps.

The boy grinned and eased his legs. They were stiff after
being braced for so long.

"No," he said. "Though I reckon you're goin' a bit far.
Mrs. Jones told me you was all set once to go to University.
Sydney, wasn't it?"

With the words came a picture of Joe tucking a bundle
of books under his arm. Joe talking, too, about things that
didn't matter, not here in the great, quiet Bush. Somehow
the picture wouldn't quite form, and he chuckled outright.

Joe said, "Yeah, it is a bit funny when yer come to look
at it. Depends on what you want, I suppose. But yer want
to remember, a little education tucked up yer sleeve doesn't
do any harm."

The colt snorted, and Joe chided it soothingly. "You
take it easy," he added, "or there'll be trouble."

The boy was quiet for moments, watching Joe's hard
brown hands on the reins. And it came to the boy that
most people's lives are hidden—especially his own, about
which no one ever asked any questions.

"Yeah," he said. "You're right, Joe. Yer need it sometimes, to get by on."

"You're dead on the nail," Joe said; then they sat in silence.

The heat from the sun, now that they were traveling more slowly, beat on the buggy. Joe seemed impervious, hunched in thought; yet his shirt was sodden. Each movement of his arms brought a ripple of wet cloth across his shoulders.

At last, after Joe had swung the horses around homeward again, the boy said, "She's a good buggy, Joe. Ole Ted did a good job. She runs as smooth as silk on the flat goin'."

Joe said, "Yeah, it's a nice outfit. There's another one in the shed old Ted's greasing. The boss wants me to give it a run, too. Maybe tomorrow, if there's nothing else doin'."

The boy rubbed his head. "So here we go," he thought. "We're off again. There's something else goin' on that nobody tells me. Just—give Joe a hand. An' that's as far as it goes. You'd reckon they'd say, or for once explain."

Aloud, he said, "Why, Joe? What are yer suddenly gettin' buggies ready for?"

He combed his fingers through his hair to let the breeze in. His scalp felt dry, burned brittle to the touch.

Joe said, "For when it rains, an' afterwards. We'll need 'em to haul stores where a car or truck would bog."

Coaxing the colt, he urged it to, "Git up in yer collar. You're loafin' on yer mate, who's doing all the pulling."

Suddenly, the colt began to kick and bolt in a series of wild, headstrong bucks that careered the buggy.

Almost tossed from his seat, the boy clung haphazardly, while Joe yelled a wild whoop, then shouted, "Go on, you beauties. Let's see what's in you. Give us a run for the final dash." And both horses complied.

Rocking and swaying, with the colt's hoofs occasionally thudding up under the dashboard, the buggy pitched and hurtled. Close to the peppercorn trees, the horses straightened into a final gallop that took them on past the woodheap.

"Lovely," Joe shouted again and again. "Come on you beauts. Come on, you flamin' beauties."

Mrs. Jones, peering quickly from the kitchen, saw only the dust drifting over the saltbush hedge. And she heard Joe's voice pitched above the buggy's rattle as it bounced behind solid, thudding hoofbeats.

Closing the door slowly, she said, "That's that crazy Joe. Sometimes I wonder what gets into him. You'd think he'd have more sense."

Alici and Maheena, who had both been outside the hedge earlier to watch the buggy leave, nodded.

Each looked at the other with careful, guarded glances before Maheena said, "Yers. 'Im crazy too much. Boss tell 'im for drive young colt. Das why all dis shout an' holler."

She pretended to be driving, shaking her body about while she held a pair of imaginary reins.

Mrs. Jones smiled. She liked the girls' playacting sometimes. It helped to relieve the monotony. So, too, did Joe's sudden wild burst of crazy yelling.

"At least," she said, "he loves what he's doing and is tough enough to take care of himself."

The two girls agreed. Both nodded their heads until their black hair danced.

And Mrs. Jones never found out that the boy had been on the buggy.

Chapter Seven

Snake from the Sky

For several days Joe drove the buggies daily, using varying pairs of horses. The boy watched and waited, hoping Joe would need him. But Joe drove alone.

From his vantage point on the woodheap, the boy noticed the colt was often unruly; yet Joe handled it without help.

"It must be me," the boy told Rags one morning. "I must've done the wrong thing."

Disconsolate, he restlessly dribbled a handful of wood chips through his fingers. Then, a sudden thought lightened his mind.

"Or maybe it ain't," he said quickly. "Maybe they reckon I've helped enough, now the colt's had 'is first run. That's it, mate, as sure as shootin'."

Relieved, he began chopping. The swing of the ax lulled him with each stroke. In the shade of a log, Rags sighed, glad that the boy was near. Both glanced around as Joe drove by, and the boy waved.

"Good goin', Joe," he called. "Thanks for the little run the other day."

If Joe heard, he took no notice. His hands and body were braced in familiar manner, and the two horses in front of him pulled head-bent on their bits.

"Lovely," the boy added. "Lovely. They look a sight, carvin' it out like that."

Unaware of a snake, stretched slim and sleek on a log, he went on chopping. Up in a peppercorn tree, a kooka-burra laughed and laughed in warning. Its beak gaped, echoing the pulse of its raucous, chuckling voice.

Looking upward, the boy shouted, "Aw, shut up. You're spoilin' the quiet."

As if in answer, the bird shook its wings, redoubling its frenzied laughter. Puzzled, the boy stared around, won-dering at the cause.

"They don't laugh for nothin'," he told Rags. "There's something about not right."

He was chopping again when the bird dived. He heard its wings slap fleetingly on the log as he whirled and stared openmouthed. His eyes felt tight, almost pushed from their sockets.

Tangled together, bird and snake were writhing and flapping one against the other. Yet he quickly saw that the bird's big beak was clamped on the snake's neck.

"You're right," he shouted, and started to run. "Jus' keep 'im nipped an' you've got 'im."

The snake wriggled fiercely to straighten its coils, and the bird seized its chance. Up it went with a driving beat of wings that lifted it into the sky. The long slim body trailed from its beak like a weaving, twisting rope. Soon the two were no more than a speck against the glare.

"Well, well, well," the boy said as he settled to watch.

"So what d'yer know? That's the second time I've seen one of 'em do that."

Alert as he always was to the rip and claw of nature, he worried for the bird. Worried, too, for the snake.

"It ain't right," he thought. "Yet what can you do? A good, clean whack on the head is one thing—or like Alici did—but t' take 'em up there an' drop 'em is another. Must be rough, floatin' down, waitin' for the ground to knock yer."

Feeling the impact, he shuddered in the heat. An icy band of cold seemed to run down his back.

Another thought came as he lowered his gaze to glance around quickly.

"What's wrong with the place?" he asked Rags questioningly. "It's only a few days since Alici killed hers, an' here's another one. I reckon it's the drought."

He remembered Kanga saying, "For every one yer see, there's a dozen out of sight."

Feeling fidgety in his feet, he stared upward again. It took several moments before he saw bird and snake poised, tiny in the sky. He barely saw the snake at all when the bird banked to let it fall. Then gradually he made out its shape as it writhed and coiled over and over.

"Fallin', fallin'," he thought, "until he hits the ground. Then the bird dives an' whips 'im up for another drop."

Barely aware of anything except the snake, he suddenly jerked his hands. They were over his eyes, shading them, while he stared, dumfounded. A whirling smother of dust almost directly under the snake made him gasp. Joe was in the dust, driving the buggy homeward.

"Aw, no," the boy whispered. "It couldn't be. Yer wouldn't see the chance in a million."

But he did. He saw the snake fall limply onto Joe's hat and Joe's sudden wild swing of his arms. For a moment the picture hung still, branded on his mind. Then the horses bolted.

Whether Joe was bitten, the boy couldn't tell. All he could see was the buggy swaying behind the two horses and Joe pitching on the seat.

Sobbing, the boy started to run. "Hold on, Joe!" he heard himself shouting. "Hold on, mate. I'm comin'."

Yet even as he shouted, he wondered what he could do —how to stop the galloping, maddened horses. Freed of Joe's firm grip, they were stretched to the limits of endurance.

"No *man* could stop 'em," was the boy's thought. "Never mind me."

Yet he urged his legs to strain faster. Their pounding seemed to him to be louder than that of the horses. Behind, he knew Rags was loping, puzzled by the strangeness of what was happening.

As the horses drew near, the boy knew he must avoid head-on impact. Between swift, jerking strides, he remembered Ross stopping a runaway team. He'd done it from the side, on a fast, trained horse.

"But me," the boy thought, "I've got nothing except me feet."

Gasping for breath, he dreaded the horror approaching, yet forced himself to meet it.

When the snorting, grunting horses were near, they suddenly shied away. The swerve almost flung Joe from the footboard, where he was desperately edging forward to climb out onto the tandem pole. One foot was already reaching between the two bolting horses' rumps.

The boy leaped and felt his hands grasp at wet, sweaty leather. Clutching with all his strength, he clung to a rein that slithered on the nearside horse's neck, while his own legs bumped on the ground.

Screaming, "Woa!" he felt his body slam and jerk until it was dragging full length at the end of his outstretched arms.

He heard Joe shout, but the words were smothered, drowned in a maelstrom of hoofs and wheels that stunned his brain.

He tried to regain his feet, but the pace was too great. His hands slipped on the sweaty-wet reins and began to slide along them. Soon he was at the end, with only a few inches of leather left in his grip. His body tossed and jerked, bumping along on the ground.

Through the mist of dust and sweat that clogged his eyes, he saw the horses were swinging, pulled by the rein he held, yet still galloping. They were pounding around him in a circle that threatened to tip the buggy. Close to him, Rags whimpered, knocked sprawling.

Almost unconscious, the boy saw Joe flung out as the buggy capsized. Then his arms and shoulders smashed against a gnarled old shrub. Through the haze engulfing him now, he felt the rein wind around and around the tough stem of the bush as the horses circled. Each time they passed him, the shortening rein scraped across his body.

Suddenly, there was darkness. The boy lay quiet, uncon-

scious in the dust. As Joe crept toward him, the horses came to a stop, straining on the rein.

From the homestead, the boss came running, followed by Mrs. Jones, Alici, and Maheena.

As they converged on Joe, he lifted the boy carefully. Staggering toward them, Joe lurched wearily.

"I'm bit," he told the boss. "But don't worry. I nicked it. Free the nags an' follow on in. The kid's had it rough an' might need a doctor."

The boss said, "Sure, keep walkin'."

Mrs. Jones steadied Joe's arm. She walked by his side while the boss and Alici stripped the horses. Maheena walked beside Joe, holding his other arm.

All three were under the peppercorn trees when the boss and Alici ran from behind to join them. Rags prowled at Joe's heels, scenting upward at the boy's tousled head.

The boss said, "I'll take 'im now, Joe."

Joe staggered on. "No," he said. "I'll get 'im to his bunk. I reckon it's best not to disturb him."

Shocked with worry, Mrs. Jones hurried ahead.

Alici followed her as the boss asked, "What did yer mean, Joe: you're bit? Bit by what?" Anxiously, he peered at the boy, trying to assess his injuries.

Joe said, "A snake. It fell on me."

The boss stared for a moment, then scuffed a hand over his chin.

"So help me," he said. "What next?"

At the hedge he held the gate open for Joe to ease the boy through. Mrs. Jones came from the kitchen with towels and hot water, and the boss took the steaming bowl from her while they followed Joe to the bunkhouse.

After putting the boy down, Joe said, "I'll leave 'im to yer for a minute. The dawg, too, had better stay, in case he wants 'im." He nodded at Rags, who had crept in unnoticed. There was utter dejection in the way he crouched on the floor.

The boss said, "Sure," and added, so that Mrs. Jones should not hear, "You get on over to the kitchen. The girls'll do something with that bite of yours. There ain't much time, whichever way you look at it."

His words expressed the thoughts worrying all of them. The nearest doctor was a hundred and fifty miles away, and probably not at home if they did try to reach him.

Joe said, "It's the way things go. They'll do as good a job as any," and left, going outside past the window.

Mrs. Jones and the boss undressed the boy and washed him. They were carefully probing every bone and muscle when he regained consciousness, to open his eyes slowly.

For a time he stared at them questioningly, puzzled at their nearness. His eyes saw them; yet it seemed unreal that they should be there, in his room.

He tried to speak, but Mrs. Jones patted his hand. "There," she smiled to say. "It's all right now."

And the boss added, "Sure. Not a bone broken or muscle pulled. You'll be up an' around in a day or two."

The boy forced himself up until he was sitting dizzily, seeing everything blur and spin.

When at last his gaze steadied, he whispered hoarsely, "Where's Joe? Did I stop 'em all right, an' was Joe bit? Did the snake get 'im?"

The dryness of his mouth parched him into silence. He sank back again, staring his unanswered question.

Mrs. Jones whispered, "What snake? He was walking when I saw him."

The boy said, "Aw, that's great. Real great," and licking his lips, looked around longingly. "I'll get up in a minute for a drink."

Mrs. Jones and the boss both moved at once.

"Lie down," Mrs. Jones murmured soothingly. "I'll get you one."

But the boss pushed past her.

"Stay here," he growled, "an' keep an eye on him. Between it all, a man don't know where he is."

Hurrying outside, he went to the kitchen. Joe was inside, hunched on a chair while Alici and Maheena bent over him. They had a tourniquet tied high on his arm, above where the snake had bitten. The gash Joe had made himself was raw and scoured.

Joe looked up to say, "They done a good job," and afterward, "How's the young bloke?"

He asked it worriedly, contrite at his own weakness. He wanted to push the girls away, strike out blindly if need be to get to the boy. But a drowsy numbness held him locked to the chair.

The boss said, "Take it quietly, Joe. He's doin' fine."

Then he asked the girls what treatment they had used while he examined Joe's arm. The cuts, slashed in a cross on the punctures, bled freely as the boss's fingers squeezed.

And as he worked, moving Joe's limbs about and asking him if he felt pain, the boss wondered. How does a man driving a buggy have a snake fall on him? Yet he asked no questions.

"They'll come later," he thought, and eased the tourni-

quet. "Right now, they don't matter. He's bitten, an' all
we c'n pray for is luck. Or maybe Joe's toughness."

Maheena explained in several short, guttural sentences
what she and Alici had done.

The boss listened intently and nodded as Maheena
ended by saying, "Now by 'n by finis'. We put 'im dis
fella plaster for make 'im good." She turned to a sauce-
pan simmering on the stove.

The boss sniffed the contents and knew them for
crushed leaves and roots pulped to a paste.

"Well," he told Joe, "it's the best there is. We couldn't
make it to a doctor in time, so what do you say? This or
Condy's crystals? Though I can tell you, that paste was
known—to the abos anyway—long before doctors were
thought of."

Joe shifted tiredly to stare at the pot. At last he drawled,
"Sure. Let 'em go, boss. They done a good job so far, so
they might as well finish it. Let 'em slap it on when they're
ready."

He closed his eyes, content just to sit with the two black
girls moving softly around him.

The boss filled a jug with water and took a glass from a
shelf. On his way to the door, he passed Maheena. She was
scraping the paste onto a piece of clean linen.

Outside, he paused for a moment before going on to the
bunkhouse.

"Some men," he said, looking down at the jug, "make
yer wonder how they do it. There ain't a blab or a bleat in
the whole of Joe's makeup."

Chapter Eight

A Dingo Howls

Despite what Mrs. Jones and the boss had said, the boy rolled off his bunk in the evening. Stiffly, he patted Rags, and the two went out together.

Above the peppercorns a flock of galahs chattered and fluttered, getting ready for the sunset. A fierce scarlet blaze was already mottling the skyline.

Ross and his men had ridden by, and the boy listened to them unsaddling at the horse yards. Their voices echoed, drifting on the hot, quiet stillness. He guessed that soon, after the boss or someone had told them, they would look for Joe, and probably him. Aching and bruised, he decided to sit on the steps without going any farther.

"Yer never know," he told Rags, "but I might get shaky, tip over, an' then where would we be? A lot more runnin' an' shoutin' while they stuffed me into bed. The best bet is to take things quietly. Sort of sneak in when it's time for dinner."

Easing downward onto a step, he stretched his legs carefully.

"They were good," he thought, "to have run like that,

belting after those horses. Or towards 'em, really. Took some doin', too, to take that jump at their heads."

He was still sitting rubbing his legs dreamily when Ross and three or four men loomed quietly near. They had been to their own quarters first and came around the bunkhouse corner. They stopped, bunched together, when they saw the boy.

Then Ross stepped forward to say, "Why ain't you in bed? We heard you were roughed up bad. The boss said you were crook, an' dam' near. . . ." He rolled a cigarette, glad he had stopped from saying "dead."

The other men nodded and chorused, "Yeah, yer did a good job," or, "Great, son. Yer did well t' stop 'em."

And Charlie, in the rear, his black face barely discernible, said, "By cri', yers. 'At's true too much. Joe tellin' everyone the way . . ." Overcome, he pushed to the front and made a mock dive, pretending to be clinging to a rein.

The others nodded again, and Ross lit the cigarette. He wasn't quite sure whether to pat the boy's shoulder or shake his hand, so decided instead to leave things just where they were, with Charlie's demonstration.

The boy grinned. "Aw," he said, "I mucked it up really. Tipped over the buggy an' everything. But it wasn't like when you stopped the mailman's horses," he told Ross. "I sort of had nothing to, er, you know, get up to 'em with," he ended lamely, rubbing his hands on his leg.

Ross said, "Sure, there's no comparison. What I did was easy. What you did, well"—he paused to glance around at the men—"it takes a good 'un, that's all I c'n say. Come on now. We'd better get some tucker."

As the men left, calling, "Good night," or "So long, an'

see yer some more," the dinner bell rang. It sounded homely, warm with the promise of plates loaded with good, tasty food, and it drew the boy like a magnet.

"Yeah," he called. "Good night, an' thanks. Tell Joe I'm better."

Ross called, "Yeah. We'll tell 'im. Now you get back to bed."

Then the quiet, still dusk was empty as the men went around the corner. To the boy, there was a sudden loneliness that made him draw Rags close.

The two sat crouched until the boy suddenly stood up. "It's no use," he told Rags. "I ain't waitin' for dinner to be brought over. It ain't the same without yer legs under that ole table."

Telling Rags to wait, he walked, limping slightly, around to the kitchen door. When he pushed it open, he heard a gasp. Mrs. Jones was serving meals onto plates, and Alici stood near, setting cutlery on a tray.

Alici stared wide-eyed as Mrs. Jones said, "My goodness, what are you doing here? I thought I told you to stay in bed."

The boy said, "Aw, I'm fine, Mrs. Jones. I was tellin' Rags that food don't taste the same when you're havin' it in bed. You sort of can't have a decent swaller, with a tray slidin' around on yer legs."

Feeling self-conscious, he edged past Mrs. Jones slowly, hoping to reach the table.

For an indecisive moment, Mrs. Jones wondered what to do—whether to send the boy back to bed or let him stay. But the pleasure of seeing him come in, in his usual manner, was too much.

Her large white hands fussed, shifting the plates, before she said, "Oh, you and your dog, telling it what you're going to do! I've never heard such rubbish. All right, Alici, set the table for him."

Maheena came in carrying a big wooden tray for the men's meals, and Mrs. Jones added, "You, too, Maheena. Don't stand staring. The plates are ready."

Yet despite her tone, there was a deft, sure happiness in her movements that was easy to see. Alici and Maheena almost danced around her in the kitchen.

Served with a dinner living up to all his imaginings, the boy ate contentedly. He wished, as he often did, that life could stand still.

"Just me," he thought, "the kitchen, an' this dinner. An' Mrs. Jones an' the girls messin' about t' see you get some more."

At last he sighed and said, "Cor! That was good, Mrs. Jones. It beats me how yer do it. There's a sort of taste that goes on an' on when you've finished eatin'."

He licked a spoon to have his last taste of pie, then pushed the plate away.

Mrs. Jones said, "You'll go on and on if you don't act sensibly. Now remember, go straight to bed and don't get up early. Someone else will cut wood in the morning. You're to have a day or two off before you start working."

With Alici and Maheena helping her, she began to tidy the kitchen. It was her pride to have everything neat and immaculate.

The boy nodded. A deep, warm flush of contentment was flooding through him. He felt tired, and the bruises ached; yet they were part of the warmth.

"Yeah," he said slowly. "I'll sleep all right, Mrs. Jones. But the trouble is in the mornin'. Yer know I like t' be up when it's fresh, like you said, an' smilin'."

He couldn't quite remember what Mrs. Jones had once quoted, but he thought his words were near enough.

Alici said, "Yers, me see 'im. S'pose me come early for light 'im fire"—she gestured at the stove—"me hear 'im. Chop, chop, or sittin' down on log, watchin' sunrise."

She gestured again, this time circling her arms so that her fingertips touched, as if she were a round red sun coming up from the earth to meet the sky. Her actions were so vivid that the boy could see the whole picture—sun, dust, and haze on a raw red skyline, while the loneliness beckoned.

"Yes," he whispered. "You got it there, Alici. I reckon you know what we mean."

Alici said, "Yers, me know. Maheena know, too."

Then the boy prepared to leave by pushing away from the table. His legs felt numbed as he stood; yet he warily forced them to move.

"If I limp," he thought, "or pull a face, they'll be on to me quick. The lot of 'em 'll be over shovin' me into bed."

Erect and stiff-legged, he walked toward the door. "Good night, Mrs. Jones," he said. "Good night, Alici an' Maheena."

He heard their murmured, almost whispered replies as he went outside. There had been a long pause, and he guessed all three were standing, watching him go.

"You could feel 'em," he told Rags later when they were both in the bunkhouse, "standin' real sharp-eyed. But it doesn't matter. I never made a slip or mistake. You wouldn't have known I was one big ache."

Rags yawned and blinked upward hopefully before crouching to leap onto the bunk, but the boy said, "No. We'll strip the sheets off first. Mrs. Jones made a good job settin' 'em on all clean an' white, but I wouldn't use 'em. Wouldn't be fair when you come to look at it."

Stripping the sheets Mrs. Jones had so carefully spread, he folded them in their creases. As he put them on the box that served him for bedside table, he wondered what to do with the sheets in the morning.

"If I take 'em over," he thought, "she'll be mad. If I don't, they'll stay 'ere an' get dusty. Whichever way it goes, there'll be a row. She'll want to know why I haven't used 'em."

Puzzling over the problem, he crawled onto the bunk. Rags leaped up beside to sprawl full length.

The two were drowsing in sleep when the soft scuffling of hoofs passing beyond the big saltbush hedge woke them.

Listening intently, the boy heard dogs pattering along as they sniffed and snuffled, yet neither whimpering nor barking. Trained dogs, held in the discipline of a large hunting pack.

Sitting up, the boy craned his neck, straining to hear the sounds. "It's Kanga," he told Rags, pulling the dog to him. "Ridin' on to the stables. He'll be a while yet tyin' his dogs an' unsaddlin', so we've got a bit of time. You can't stay here, that's certain. He'd tear down the place if he saw you."

Pulling on his boots, the boy hobbled stiffly outside

again. With Rags at his heels, he headed for the little feed shed. On the way, he explained to Rags why they were moving—or at least why Rags was being taken to the little shed.

"Ole Kanga's tough," the boy said, limping painfully for a moment and remembering the past, "an' he expects dogs to be even tougher. Their place, he says, is working, or tied to a peg. Never in a house, or even near one."

As he talked, the boy could see the pack; see Skipper, the "king" dog, and Kanga's gaunt, lined face poised above his giant old frame. The darkness framed the pictures that came vividly to his mind. It was almost as if he could reach out to touch Kanga's gnarled brown hand.

"If I did," the boy added, more to himself than Rags, "he'd belt me one. Knock me sprawling. Yet he's gettin' better at having a talk. Like last time when he was home. We had some good yarns then about things—especially Roany's hoof."

At the shed he shut Rags inside and waited for Kanga. He knew the old dogman would have to pass by. Presently, a tall, wide figure loomed, and the boy moved forward. Side by side, the two walked on toward the woodheap.

Neither spoke until at last the boy said, "You're late, Kanga, ain't you? I mean, yer often come in late, I know, but not as late as this."

He gestured around at the darkness that seemed to be pressing in. Even the logs of the woodheap were barely visible as the boy and Kanga stepped around them.

Near the gate in the hedge, Kanga paused to light his pipe. As the match flared, he peered over the pipe's bowl, first at the boy, then slowly around at the bare, dusty ground.

"Where's the dawg?" he asked, and as he tossed the spent match down, he added, "Why are yer limpin'? You were bobbin' about comin' across, like a horse with its leg broken."

He strode on again without waiting for an answer. There was a slow, weathered certitude in the way he moved through the darkness. His hands neither bumped nor fumbled when he opened the gate.

"So," the boy thought, limping on with the old dogman toward the bunkhouse, "he's noticed. But it doesn't matter. He'd have seen me, or found out in the mornin' anyway. Joe or someone is sure to tell 'im."

Halting at the steps, he said, "Rags is in the shed. I put 'im there in case he strayed near Skipper. An' another thing, Kanga. The colt's real good. Roany, as I call 'im, is doin' fine. You wouldn't think there was ever anything wrong with his hoof."

Kanga puffed his pipe slowly. Tall on the ground, he towered taller than ever from where he stood on the steps, yet only as a shadow that the boy saw loom below the glowing pipe bowl.

The pipe dulled as Kanga took it from his mouth to say, "You've said about the dawg, an' brought in the horse. Now where's the rest of it?"

Kanga sat down on the doorstep, resting his shoulders against a door jamb. The boy saw the pipe glow again as the old man jabbed it back into his mouth.

Squatting down to ease his legs, the boy told Kanga about Joe, the snake, and the bolting horses. With his arms looped around his knees, he tried to explain his own part but felt he was boasting.

"Whichever way you talk," he thought during a temporary silence, "it sounds like skitin'. Blowin' yerself up into a big balloon of nothing."

He was glad when finally he said, "So there it is, Kanga. I got dragged into a bush an' then flaked out. The whole lot went as black as this night is."

His body had stiffened, and he pushed himself upright inch by inch. A pain in his back made him almost flop down again.

Kanga said, "The way it went, you were lucky. Joe was, too. The main thing is there's nothing broken. A bruise or two'll go as they came—suddenly." Then he added as the boy followed him into the bunkhouse, "I've bin eighty years knockin' around the Bush, but never seen a snake fall on a man. That's something you've beaten me to." And for the first time, the boy thought he detected a chuckle in Kanga's voice.

Pleased, the boy went into his own room and pulled off his boots. Sprawled flat on the bunk, he stared up at the ceiling. Through the thin wall that divided his room from Kanga's, he heard the old dogman light a lantern. The soft yellow glow filtered beyond the open doorway.

"So there yer are," the boy thought, yawning. "He's home, an' it's great to see him. That ole pipe of his sort of makes the place right. Different to the usual smell you get from these knotty pine planks. I bet they were sawn when he was about my age, or maybe younger. It's hard to imagine, but there it is."

The boy tried, but he couldn't imagine or see Kanga

young; couldn't see the giant old frame brought down to his own size. Stare through the darkness as he would, nothing came except Kanga's tall, weathered form and gaunt, seamed face.

Feeling sleep creep over him, the boy yawned again. In the next room, Kanga heard the sound as he blew out the light. Then there was complete and utter silence except for the boy's heavy breathing.

Kanga lay as if his body were clamped to the mattress; yet his eyes stayed open, gazing upward. He tried to see what the boy had tried to see and instead saw only the warm, still darkness.

In the early dawn before light, the boy awoke to the creak of footsteps. Peering from his blankets, he saw Kanga creep past the open door. As the old dogman paused outside to light his pipe, a dingo howled, sobbing beyond the peppercorns.

"That's rare," the boy thought, sitting up. "Yer don't often hear 'em. Not so close to the homestead, anyway." And as he sat rubbing the soreness in his legs, he wondered what Kanga was thinking.

Then he heard Kanga saying, "Now where did he come from? I thought that area was clean."

Sliding from his bunk, the boy limped across to the window. Kanga was standing not far from the sill with his head bent, listening; waiting, the boy guessed, for another howl from the dingo. But none came.

After several minutes Kanga strode off, padding lightly on the dust, until the gate slammed shut behind him. At its noisy thud, some sleepy galahs in the peppercorns began complaining.

"Aw," the boy said. "Go back to sleep."

Testing his legs and arms, then prodding his ribs and body, he moved around the room slowly. Gradually, he decided that most of the bumps and bruises felt easier.

"With a bit of luck," he told himself, pulling on his boots, "I'll be over the worst today. But Ross'll be mad if he sees me on the woodheap. He's bound to get Charlie or one of 'em to cut a load or two."

The words, as he muttered them, reminded him of the ax. His remembrance was that he had thrown it down before running toward Joe and the bolting horses.

"As like as not," he thought, stomping his boots to make them fit, "it's still lyin' there. But I'd better check, just in case. Yer never know. I might've slung it in among the logs."

He found the ax and wedged it into a log where it could be seen. Restless at not having work to do, he almost decided to follow Kanga, then changed his mind. He knew Kanga would be in the blacksmith's shop, boiling a billy for tea—yet the restlessness was too strong.

"A mug of tea," he told Rags when he freed him from the shed, "would be great. So would a yarn with Kanga. But I reckon a walk will tread off some of this stiffness."

Bending as he spoke to brush some straw from Rags, he felt a pain twinge his back. "An' there," he added, straightening slowly, "is a bit of it. The stiffness, I mean. You were lucky yesterday; you didn't get bumped about as much as me. That ole flyer really belted me into the dust."

With the memory revived vividly in his mind, he trudged away from the shed and on under the peppercorns. Rags followed, content in the grayish half-light to see the outline of the boy. There was pleasure, too, in the way the young dog sometimes sniffed at the heels that occasionally lurched in front of it, for try as he would, the boy couldn't avoid limping if his feet tramped over uneven ground. More than once he paused to rest, disgusted with himself.

And each time he said down to Rags, "You see, I'm mad. Like Mrs. Jones says, I ought t' be in bed. An' if I had any brains, I would be."

Following on this argument, he wondered why he did some things. The mystery was something he couldn't answer, and he trudged on thinking of other things while the dawn came angrily on the skyline. A great sheet of flame seemed to be eating at the grayness.

Feeling the heat already flowing around him, the boy scuffed his face. Close to some scrub, he sat down for a moment to rest his legs and open his shirt front. As the dry, stifling air reached his chest, he stared around thoughtfully.

"Yer know," he told Rags, "it's somewhere around here I heard that dingo howl. An' another thing"—he shaded his eyes carefully to see better—"ole Kanga's on the move. I c'n see him behind the stables saddlin' his horse. Old Skipper's near 'im, standing by the dog pack."

Lowering his hands, the boy stared around again intently. Rags had suddenly bristled into a fierce, silent watchfulness. His whole body trembled, but he made no sound. And the boy saw the young dog was scenting, keen-nosed to the motionless air, sifting the vagrant odors down to one invisible thing: the dingo, or maybe several dingoes.

The boy had heard they sometimes ran in pairs or even

packs. The lone howl could have been one calling to another or a leader summoning his pack.

Feeling his neck tingle at the thought, the boy struggled up to his feet. Trudging on, he searched the ground in front of him for paw marks. They would have shown easily, he reckoned, on the smooth red dust. He saw lizard, bird, and snake tracks, but no sign of any elusive dingo.

He was thinking of returning to the homestead and a mug of hot steaming tea in the kitchen when he saw a shape. Then another, and another. Three altogether, he counted. Wispy, reddish shapes, loping some distance away through a patch of withered tussock grass.

As the boy whispered, "Cor! Look at 'em, will yer!" three more appeared, and he knew them for dingoes. Six lean, muscled animals, honed by their existence to a razor-sharp intelligence and a wariness that blended them with the ground.

Several times the boy scuffed his eyes to make sure they weren't deceiving him. Sometimes he saw the shapes; sometimes there was only the thin, spiky grass. But Rags saw them more with his nose than his eyes. Creeping at the boy's heels, he held his head rigid. His nostrils scented every weave and twist of the slinking, fading shapes.

At last they were gone, merged suddenly into the wide brown quietness. No twig, leaf, or stem quivered to show their passing, and as the boy gazed, trying to catch one more fleeting glimpse, he wheeled to a sound. It was the shrill, high trill of Kanga's piercing whistle. And in answer to it came the deep, throbbing bay of his dog pack searching for the dingoes.

When they found the scent, the pack converged, held

banded by old Skipper, and ran in a solid phalanx of eager, jostling bodies. Kanga rode in their rear, as if welded to the saddle of the big bay horse he rode.

Neither Kanga nor the dogs took notice of the boy or Rags as they passed. Their whole concentration awed the boy by its deadly sense of purpose.

"They ain't seein' us," he told Rags, "or the blood-red sun or nothing. Just smellin' the tracks of something they're trained to kill. An' it makes you wonder, seein' it. You can't sort of figure the whys an' wheres."

While he spoke, he held the young dog clutched against him. Rags was vibrant with longing to follow the questing, hunting pack, and the boy chided soothingly.

Sitting down with Rags in his arms, the boy wondered at instincts—especially the age-old one of hunting. "It's stronger in some," he thought, "than in others. Especially in men like Kanga."

He shrugged, baffled by the thoughts swirling around in his mind. One part of him wanted to join in the hunt with Kanga; the other half couldn't stand the thought of those red, slinky shapes being brought to bay—seeing their wild, stubbly-eared heads torn to ribbons by the pack.

"Yet they hunt, too," he told Rags in continuance of the argument wrestling in his mind. "An' some of the cruelty they get up to don't bear thinking about. So you could more or less say it's fair to destroy 'em."

Feeling he was more or less where he had started, the boy freed Rags and started to walk.

"Come on," he added. "We'll get back to the woodheap. Or come to think of it, breakfast. We're a bit late now for a mug of tea or even t' look in on Roany."

Thought of the colt brought the boy back to his own present state—that of a sore and bruised body still twinging with aches and pains.

"Yet I'm lucky," he said, staring straight ahead to the peppercorns. "Dead lucky. Nobody says much, but they get on with doing my job. Charlie's cuttin' wood, an' someone else will feed the horses. Work's goin' on in the same old way; yet I'm doing nothing."

The thought, put into words, worried him. His hands itched for the ax or a bucket or a pitchfork—anything rather than be hanging loosely by his sides. To ease his sense of uselessness, he glanced behind, hoping to see the impossible: Kanga riding home, leading a dog pack tail-hung in defeat. But the great brown folds of scrub and plain stretched emptily to the skyline. Kanga, dogs, and dingoes were hidden in the vastness. A curtain of haze hung on the silent Bush.

"It's as if he was swallowed," the boy told Charlie when he reached the woodheap. "You can't see or hear 'im anywhere. Do yer reckon he caught 'em or that maybe they got away?"

He ended flatly, with a pretended note of indifference in his voice. Glad for the chance, he sat stiffly on a log. His feet seemed numbed, stifled in his boots.

Charlie lowered the ax, pleased to rest from the unusual work of chopping. Two mounds of split wood stood near him, and he squatted down on one of them.

"Yeah," he said. "By cri' me think 'im true. Dis fella dingo got 'im brain for savvy." He screwed up his face and eyelids in a watchful, wary manner and distended his broad, flat nostrils as if scenting. "You see 'im like dis, der next minute 'e gone. Gone flitterin' like the shadows when der sun come up." With slow, gentle movements, he pantomimed with his hands, showing the boy how shadows disappear.

The boy nodded, unconvinced by Charlie's words or actions that the dingoes had escaped. The two stared quietly for a moment, peering into the distances.

Then the boy said, "Well, I reckon they might have gone at that. There were six of 'em, Charlie. Six red, slinky fellers prowlin' along in the dust."

Charlie hissed through his teeth, then spat thoughtfully. "By cri' . . ." he started to say when the garden gate banged open and Maheena stood beckoning.

There was a soft kind of scolding in her voice as she

called, "Missus say where you stop? She got breakfas' for you all ready an' waitin'."

The boy slid to his feet. Charlie scrambled up to reach for the ax.

The two glanced again toward the horizon before the boy said, "Yeah, I'd reckon I better go. If yer see anything, you c'n tell me afterwards. Come on, Rags. You can stretch out by the gate."

With the dog at his heels, he limped, stiff after sitting, across to Maheena. She held the gate open while he brushed past to go through.

Nearing the kitchen, Maheena said, "Missus cross li'le bit, she no find 'em you still in bed. She say you silly for walk with all dem bruises." To emphasize what she meant, she clutched her hip and began to limp, dragging one foot in the dust.

The boy grinned. "Go on," he said. "You an' Charlie make a good pair. But I'm sorry about Mrs. Jones. I'll bet she *was* mad at not finding me in bed."

Maheena said, "Yers, she mad all right," and after they reached the kitchen, hesitated before walking away.

"She wants to stay," the boy thought, "an' see how things go—sort of be around in whatever's doin'—yet can't because of another job."

But in the kitchen, Mrs. Jones smiled when she saw him. The usual damp-ringed look of heat and tiredness was on her face, though she moved briskly.

"I might have known," she said, setting his breakfast on the table, "you'd be up if it killed you. And why on earth didn't you use the sheets? What kind of bee is it that gets into you?"

Fighting her exasperation, she made a fresh pot of tea while the boy sat down at the table.

"Aw," he said. "You know how it is, Mrs. Jones."

Then, at a loss for anything further to say, he filled his mouth with food. At least he couldn't be expected to talk while eating.

Mrs. Jones scraped a pan. "Yes," she said. "If I don't now, I never will. Yet the strange thing is, I don't believe I do."

This enigmatic answer baffled the boy. Bent over, he drank a great gulp of tea. Outside, far off in the distance, he thought he heard a dog pack baying. But it was only a thought that swirled with the dregs in his cup.

He reached for the pot at the same time as Mrs. Jones. There was understanding in the way she pushed away his fingers.

Chapter Nine

Maheena's Mistake

That afternoon Joe was wandering around searching for the boy when he found him in Roany's stall. Rags was there, too, sprawled on the freshly raked straw. Joe saw the colt outlined by the sun streaming fiercely through the shutters. By its side the boy leaned awkwardly, grooming the glossy flanks.

For a moment Joe wondered whether to enter as he pushed open the stall door. Then the boy looked up.

"Cor," he said, and slid a hand over Roany's rump. "It's good t' see yer, Joe. I heard you were fine, though it's not like seein' you. I went over to your quarters this mornin', but you wasn't there."

Hoping Joe might stay for a yarn, he gave the colt a final pat before squatting down in a corner. Rags followed him, lazily crawling through the straw.

Joe said, "Yeah, I was doin' some washing. The boss told me to take a day off, so I thought I'd catch up on a shirt or two."

Laconic as always, Joe took a few paces and eased himself down to a position where he could study the colt before he added, "But you know how it is. A man gets bored just moonin' around doin' nothing."

He gave a shrug that nearly split the shirt on his shoulders. His face showed disgust, and he pulled at the bandage padded on his arm as if eager to tear it off.

The boy nodded. There was a universal evasiveness about Joe's expression, "But you know how it is," that reminded him of the morning; of Mrs. Jones' baffled retort and his own inarticulate explaining.

"Joe's stuck like me," he thought, "with nothing to do or say. He'd like to talk about what's happened but chokes up. So instead, he just sort of drops in to pass the time of day an' see how things are. Tomorrow he'll be first one across to the horse yards, waitin' for Ross an' the rest of 'em."

Thought of Ross made the boy say, "He didn't go crook or anything—Ross, I mean—about the buggy or horses. All I heard that he said was that luck was with us. An' I reckon it was, Joe. Not a wheel or spoke broken, or even a horse cut. Makes yer think, when you remember how they were belting."

He suddenly shivered, remembering the flying, pounding hoofs thudding nearer and nearer. The horses seemed magnified to massive proportions.

Joe saw the shiver and guessed at the cause. "Well," he said. "That's as maybe. An' I reckon Ross didn't mean it quite like yer say." He paused to add emphasis. "Nor do I. So"—he paused again and stood up—"if ever you're stuck or short of a quid, or short of anything for that matter, you know where to come. From this hat to me boot heels, you c'n have the lot."

With the hat dragged from his head in one hand, he strode quickly from the stalls. A loud clatter echoed throughout the stables when he kicked a bucket flying.

"So there it is," the boy told Rags after a long, thoughtful silence. "He's been bustin' to say it an' finally did. Now he'll be as right as rain next time we see 'im. Won't say a word except the usual things, an' from now on he'll reckon it's up to me."

Rags yawned, and the boy, chuckling over Joe's storming exit, began to bed down and feed the stabled horses. Afterward he went outside to climb stiffly onto the topmost rails of the horse yards.

There seemed to be more than the usual haze spread around the westering sun, though after his first assessing glance, he turned to gaze eastward.

Soon, he made out the dusty swirl of Ross and his men riding homeward. Then, still peering intently, he saw another rider some distance beyond the stockmen. It was Kanga, trailed by his weary dog pack and barely seen against the harsh, bare background.

As the riders neared, the boy slid down and trudged across to the woodheap. On the way he shut Rags in the little feed shed.

"While Kanga's home," he told the young dog before closing the door, "you'll have to suffer it. If ole Skipper got at you. Well. . . ." He shrugged and walked on, talking to himself: "There'd be real trouble. The only one who could stop it would be Kanga, an' he mightn't be around."

Reaching the woodheap, he saw Maheena was already there, sitting in the wheelbarrow. One hand held an ax,

the other, the legs of three headless chickens. Their severed heads were lying near the aboriginal girl's feet.

As the boy suddenly stopped, she said, "Me kill 'im
chicken. Missus Jones say for find 'im someone, but me no
find 'im. So"—she flicked a speck of blood from her leg—
"me kill 'im."

The boy stared. One of the chickens was the young
rooster he had particularly cared for. He knew it by its
wing tips. They were reddy-gold, flecked against white.
Some time before, he had made arrangements with Joe,
who did the Yamboorah butchering, not to kill the bird.
Instead, it would be kept for breeding. Now here it was,
hanging dead in Maheena's hands.

For some moments the boy gazed, as if not comprehend-
ing. Then he felt a kind of fullness that choked him.

When at last his throat freed, he shouted, "What did yer
want to kill 'im for? There's another dozen in the pen, but
you had to pick him. Cor, I dunno, it makes me sick. You
know I wanted to keep 'im."

Angrily, he hobbled over to stare down at the chickens'
heads. He wished there was some way he could put them
back, so the young rooster would be whole again.

Then he saw Maheena's face. Tears wreathed through
the misery that filled her eyes, and she slumped limply.
Slowly, the chickens slid from her hands to fall in the dust.
With one great sob, she scrambled from the barrow and
started to run.

Sniffling through her tears, she called back over her
shoulder, "No find 'im Joe. No find 'im anyone. Me no
savvy you want 'im dis fella chicken."

Sobbing heartbreakingly, she doubled around and ran past the boy toward the stables.

A slam from the garden gate told him someone else was coming, but he was already running—or trying to. His legs felt jerky and stiff and almost uncontrollable. Every aching step nearly brought him down flat on his face. Scuffling along, he saw Maheena head for the blacksmith's shop.

He started to shout, "Hey, wait a minute, Maheena," when he glanced around to see Alici at his shoulder.

After a quick, fleeting look at the boy's face, she asked, "What's the matter dis place? Why Maheena run?"

The boy stumbled. Staggering along to regain his feet again, he shouted, "She killed a chicken, an' I went crook. Then she bolted. Why?" He shrugged in full stride. "I dunno. Though I reckon I was mad to get shoutin' at 'er. She didn't know."

Sucking in his breath, he bent his arms for a fresh effort. And as he spurted, he found his movements were getting easier. Some of the stiffness was leaving his muscles.

"Just goes to show," he thought, "how things c'n go. If I'd have stayed in bed, I'd still be as stiff as a board."

Pleased, he hoped to stay pace for pace with Alici, but she quickly drew away from him. Running loosely, without apparent effort, she literally swirled at every stride. Her skirts tossed and bobbed, pounded by her black, shining knees.

"Phew!" the boy gasped, trying to gain an inch or two. "If she's as hot as I am, I bet the sweat's runnin' off 'er."

But Alici neither eased her pace nor faltered. A few yards beyond the blacksmith's shop, she drew abreast of Maheena and caught her around the waist. The two seemed to struggle for a moment, then Maheena relaxed, to rest her head on Alici's shoulder.

The two were standing together when the boy came close. Needing time to get his breath, as well as to wipe the sweat from his streaming face and neck, he sat on the hub of an old wagon wheel.

Presently, Alici told Maheena to, "Stop dis fella silly business," and they both sat down opposite the boy on upturned kerosene tins. The fiercely hazed sun, flaring miraged on the sandhills behind them, gave a reddish tint to their black limbs and faces.

"Like copper," the boy thought, "when it's old an' polished. Though they ain't old. The way they run, you'd reckon they had springs, not legs."

Scuffing his face for a final time, he said, "We're out of sight here. Ross an' his men won't see us as they unsaddle. They're not too far off now if you ask me."

He hoped to sound indifferent while he wondered what to say to Maheena. She still had the downcast look on her face. What puzzled the boy was that she was usually a calm, steady girl who could smile at most things.

Then suddenly he thought he had the answer. He remembered how recently Alici had nearly succumbed to the urge of "walkabout." Maybe, in a different way, Maheena was being pulled by the same impulse. One little upset over the chickens was enough to cause a flood of nervy emotions.

Relieved, the boy stood up to walk over to Maheena.

"Sorry," he said, "for shoutin' out like I did. An' the rooster don't matter, anyway. He had to go some time."

Rubbing his head, he went back to sit on the wheel hub again. He was glad, when he glanced across, to see that Maheena's face had lightened. Alici, too, was smiling.

"Yers," Maheena nodded to say. "Me sorry, too. Sorry too much. Something stop along dese fingers me no savvy." She held up her hands, staring at them intently. "Dey kill 'im rooster all the same friend for you." She sighed, wishing she hadn't made the mistake, and Alici patted her arm.

The boy said, "Aw, it wasn't that bad. In fact, nothing like it. Yer know I feed 'em all from chicks, an' he sort of took to me more than the others. Used to hop on to me wrist for an extra snack or anything that was goin'. So there it is. It's over now."

He paused thoughtfully, seeing momentarily the young,

sleek rooster fluttering on his wrist. "He's gone, an' there's
an end. We'd better get on before there's a row. Mrs.
Jones'll be worried if you're not there soon."

At mention of Mrs. Jones, Alici said, "Yers, she send
me for look 'im Maheena."

The boy chuckled, and when he stood up, he saw that
Ross and his men were just riding up to the saddle shed.

"Hold on a bit," he told the girls, "an' we c'n slip across
unnoticed. Or better still, go round by the vehicle shed."

He pointed, and Maheena and Alici nodded, eager now
to get back to Mrs. Jones.

At the woodheap the chickens lay as Maheena had
dropped them, limp-feathered in the dust. She picked
them up by their yellow legs and, without looking at the
boy, followed Alici to the garden gate, then on to a meat-
house set behind the homestead.

"So there we are," the boy said, sitting down on a log.
"That's the end of them. An' I kicked up a row. But
where's the sense? All it did was to make 'er bust out cryin'.
Just that, an' nothing more. You can't say sorry an' put
their heads back on, once an ax has lopped 'em."

Reminded of the heads, he buried them before Ross arrived with his men.

As they passed, they nodded or called, "How are yer
now?" or, "See you're back on yer castle." And Ross, in
the lead, paused to say, "Why all the runnin'? What was
the corroboree between you an' them girls?"

Ross asked the question indifferently, staring beyond
the boy to Kanga, now drawing nearer. Ross's face, the
boy suddenly noticed—as if seeing it for the first time—
was haggard. Tired to a gauntness that reminded him of

Kanga. And the boy guessed that worry was the major cause.

"It's the drought," he thought. "An' the troubles that go with it. Must be things goin' on every day that I wouldn't dream of. Cattle bogged in dryin' waterholes—crows peckin' the eyes from weak, but still livin' calves." He shivered, feeling the sweat go cold on his neck.

Yet the boy knew that he himself was somehow cut off from the main world of Yamboorah. Except for the enormous panoramic vistas he could see from the windmill top, he had never been beyond a twelve- or fifteen-mile radius from the homestead. And that, he knew, was only a fraction of the great, isolated cattle property.

It was out in the distant areas that the drought was really causing disaster. The area around the homestead was not so heavily stocked. Mostly it was used for the big herds of Yamboorah horses. If these were not kept in reasonable condition, all work would stop on the property.

These fleeting thoughts reacted on the boy. His mind tried to grasp the reality of the lives the men near him led. The harsh, raw savagery of drought, heat, and dust they could seemingly shrug off easily. Yet he wondered if, like him, they had some softness.

Suddenly, realizing he was staring wide-eyed at Ross, he said, "Aw, yeah, that was about some chickens. Joe wasn't around t' kill some for the kitchen."

Ross said, "Oh! Is that what it was?" and, striding on, talked softly with the men until the gate slammed behind them all.

Left on his own, the boy watched Kanga ride past to the stables. The dog pack panted, wide-jawed from a long day

in the heat. Seeing their slavering tongues, the boy wondered about the dingoes. Were they like the roosters, lying
somewhere, dead? Not wanting to ask, he trudged to his
room quickly.

"Whichever way you look," he thought, stretching out
on his bunk, "there's strife an' trouble. An' I suppose the
main thing is weather. You get tied up in it, whichever
way you turn."

He heard Kanga come in and light his lamp. The fiery-
hazed sun had gone, leaving a reddish-gray twilight that
was quickly fading to darkness.

As it deepened, Kanga clumped about in his room before he finally called, "It's close up t' bell time. They'll be
ringin' it in a minute."

He came along the little hall to stand in the boy's doorway, looking down.

The boy said, "Yeah, Kanga. An' I could do with a
feed."

Sliding from his bunk, he went outside with the old
dogman, and they waited quietly, standing on the doorstep. A last flurry of galahs flapped, slapping their wings
in the peppercorns.

"They're late," the boy told Kanga. "Must've been a
long way, searchin' for something to nibble. They don't
look as shiny as they used to."

While he spoke, the dinner bell rang. Side by side with
Kanga, he began walking along the path.

At the corner where Kanga had to take the branching
path that led to the men's quarters, the old dogman paused
to say, "No, an' they're lucky to be where they are. Out
where I bin, they're down to skin an' feathers."

Leaving the boy, he stalked on without looking back. There was a crunching from his boots when the path changed to gravel.

The boy trudged on, too. The hazy night seemed heavier than he ever remembered. Even the stars couldn't break clearly through the dead, cloying atmosphere.

In the kitchen, Mrs. Jones turned to smile when he pushed open the door. There was an eagerness in the way he closed the door behind him that warmed Mrs. Jones— as if he were shutting out something he wanted to hide or leave behind in the darkness.

"Hello," she said, then asked him how he was while she forked pumpkin onto the plate in front of her.

The savory smell made the boy's mouth water, and suddenly the warm, strong comfort of food gushed over him.

He could barely talk clearly as he said, "Aw, I'm good thanks, Mrs. Jones. Me legs feel fine."

He jiggled them to show her how good they were before he sat down at the table.

As he ate, he felt almost as if he shouldn't. And the thought came that no matter how many doors he closed, he could never again shut out the drought or its sorrow. It was with him now, as it was with all the others on Yamboorah, until rain came, bringing relief.

"It makes you think," he suddenly mumbled to Mrs. Jones, with his mouth full. "Or I should say, wonder. You can't sort of see where it's all going to end."

Mrs. Jones stared, trying to form a picture of what the boy meant.

At last, she said, "Oh, you mean the drought. Well, it doesn't do any good, does it? Neither thought nor talk can bring what's needed. Only a break in this dreadful weather can do that."

She lifted a pot from the stove, and the boy watched her, pretending to be absorbed in eating. Her hands seemed to have lost some of their firmness, but he wasn't sure. Her eyes, too, worried him. The continually damp, dark rings around them seemed to be growing larger.

"An' if they are," he thought, "it's the weather again. She's in here day after day, an' the heat comin' at her all ways. Yer wouldn't reckon she could keep it up much longer."

He wiped his plate with a piece of bread, then pushed it away. With the taste of gravy rich in his mouth, he waited for a helping of pie.

As Mrs. Jones set it down in front of him, Alici came in, followed by Maheena. They bustled about, but the boy noticed they were glancing sometimes at him, sometimes at Mrs. Jones. The glances were quick and meant to be hidden by the furtive lowering of their eyelashes. Yet he saw them easily and wondered if Mrs. Jones could, or whether she sensed the girls were on edge. He guessed they were wondering whether he had told Mrs. Jones anything about the chickens.

As if prompted by his thoughts, Mrs. Jones suddenly said, "What's the matter with you two? Anyone would think you'd been up to something."

The two girls smiled and shook their heads.

"They reckon," the boy thought, staring at their black, shining faces, "that I haven't told her anything, or she wouldn't have asked what she did."

Spooning some pie, he almost chuckled when Alici said, "No, missus. No up to something."

Though when she added, "By 'n by close up now, you see," his forehead wrinkled in puzzlement. He wasn't quite so sure he knew the reason for their manner or their glances.

Mrs. Jones said, "All right. Be mysterious if you want to," and poured herself a cup of tea.

Still smiling, the two girls moved about around her, tidying plates and saucepans, ready to wash them in the sink.

Later, sitting on the bunkhouse steps waiting for Kanga, the boy rubbed his head. The deep, threatening stillness had grown darker and closer; yet there were no clouds. The stars showed, dimmed from their usual glory to smudged blurs of light. Gazing up at them, the boy pondered over the evening, over the day, and other preceding days.

"Somehow," he thought, "it can't go on. There has to be an end somewhere. An' I reckon this haze has the answer. You c'n feel it, but nobody's sayin' anything, in case it goes wrong." Though Alici had given a hint when she'd said, "By 'n by close up now, you see."

Drawing up his knees, he sat waiting till Kanga came. There was a quietness then between them that suited the night's hushed sounds and the steady glowing bowl of Kanga's pipe.

Chapter Ten

Skipper Leads the Way

The morning dawned, speared with a savage redness. Again the haze was turned to a purplish scarlet flare that throbbed with heat. Clumping stiffly across to the little feed shed, the boy gazed around at the barely outlined buildings.

"You'd think," he told Rags after the shed door was opened, "that they were on fire. Look at 'em! Glowin', you might say, an' the sun ain't even up. It's got to bust some time or we'll all sizzle."

Rags stretched, glad to be near the boy again, and the two went back to the woodheap, where the boy searched about for his ax.

When he found it, he began to chop wood. His limbs and body still felt sore, but after a few strokes the muscles seemed to ease. Pleased that he was once more able to work, he swung happily and barely heard the garden gate slam.

Light-footed in his thin-soled riding boots, Wirranoona strode by on his way to the horse yards. Passing the boy, he nodded to say the usual, "Good day," and continued on his way.

A few moments later another slam of the gate heralded Charlie, who shouted, "Hey! Which way along you fella? Ross say for me cut 'im wood. You sore too much for two or t'ree days." Hurrying close to the boy, he attempted to take the ax.

The boy said, "Aw, I'm right, Charlie. But thanks all the same. You tell Ross I'm as good as new."

To add conviction, he drove the ax down in a neat, swinging blow that completely split a block.

Charlie stood scratching his head until at last he decided there was no sense in staying.

"O.K.," he said. "Me tell 'im Ross. One way, 'nother way, I reckon 'e glad. You savvy we got 'im plenty work."

In quick, pantomiming actions, he pretended to be riding a horse and peering anxiously across the vast landscape.

Leaning on the ax, the boy noticed how the aboriginal's broad nose distended while his eyelids narrowed to wrinkled slits. The senses of sight and smell were so intertwined that he couldn't use one without the other. And, the boy guessed, it's the same with his hearing.

"I'll bet he's sniffing, hearing, an' seeing all together," he thought.

Aloud, he said, "Yeah, that's what I reckoned, Charlie. So you don't have to worry. You push off now an' see to whatever you have to."

Charlie left, sucking his teeth with pleasure at not having to chop wood, while the boy again hefted his ax.

He had a barrowful of wood cut by the time Wirranoona, straddled on the bare-backed night horse, drove the galloping saddle horses he had mustered into the horse yards. Watching the dust swirl above the jostling animals, the boy felt thankful to be working again in his old routine.

"It was only a day," he told Rags, trundling the barrow steadily toward the gate and on to the kitchen. "Or yer could say, two days. Because it was early when I got busted. An' I tell you something. It's funny how long it seems. You'd reckon I'd been crook for weeks, not just a day or two."

He left Rags at the gate and trundled on, whistling. The pleasant sound of eggs spitting softly as they fried came through the gauze door when he stopped. Gathering an armful of wood, he shouldered into the kitchen feeling glad to be alive—happy, almost to the point of shouting.

Dumping down the wood to its place in the woodbox, he said, "Good mornin', Mrs. Jones. Sounds great to hear 'em if you're passin' outside. The eggs, I mean," he added, nodding down at the pan on the stove. "They sort of spit cheerily, sayin', 'Come an' eat me quick.' "

Lost for more words and suddenly thinking that those he had said sounded silly, he wheeled to go outside for another armful.

Mrs. Jones said, "That's lovely. I never quite thought of it that way. Eggs always seem to spit, and yes, they do sound happy. Well I never, you've made my day."

Humming, she bent over the eggs to push a slice under them and stop them from sticking.

The boy stopped long enough to say, "Aw, I'm glad of

that, Mrs. Jones," but outside he paused for a moment, wonderingly.

Mrs. Jones looked brighter and fresher than he had seen her for a long time. Yet only yesterday she had been as depressed as he had been over the heat and drought.

Peering around at the hazed, raw sky, he could find no answer, except to mumble to himself as he gathered another big armful of wood, "I'm the same. I feel as different as them chickens would've done if I could've shoved their heads back on."

Reminded of the chickens, he wondered which one he would get a slice of when it came to dinnertime. Common sense argued with his innate sentimentality all the time he was eating breakfast.

When evening came, the boy was thinking of other things. So was Mrs. Jones and everyone else on Yamboorah. Great drops of rain were falling with strange regularity from a blackened, brooding sky. Not driving sheets of drops, but huge single drops that plopped leadenly on dust, corrugated iron roofs, trees, and shrubs.

Hunched in the stall with Roany and Rags, the boy listened to the ploppings. At first they seemed unreal, and so did the sky with its awful covering of darkness. The light coming through was eerily dim, outlining only the nearest objects.

"If this keeps up," he told Rags, "it'll be dark in another hour. Pitch dark. You won't be able to see an inch in front of yer. I'll bet Ross an' Kanga an' the rest of 'em are beltin' it out to get home. Yet the funny thing is . . ."

He paused and, after giving Roany a final pat, went outside with Rags. "Just look at it," he continued. "The rain, I mean. You could count every drop an' watch it land. They're as big as pumpkins, too," he added, baffled into exaggeration by the rain's strangeness.

That night Kanga wasn't home when the dinner bell rang, and the boy worried as he trudged through the rain to the kitchen. He had seen Ross and his men arrive, all of them sodden from the listless, heavy drops. But Kanga, inscrutable, tough, unyielding as always to the normal routine of others, hadn't arrived. The boy wondered at a perverseness that could keep a man from food and shelter on such a night.

He shivered as he entered the kitchen, and Mrs. Jones misunderstood. "Yes," she said, "your shirt is sopping. Why don't you put something round your shoulders?"

And the words were barely spoken before she remembered the boy's room. When she had tidied it recently, there was no sign of either a coat or covering that could be used in bad weather. Her concern showed plainly as she served the boy's dinner.

But the boy shrugged stiffly. "Aw, it's not that, Mrs. Jones," he told her. "I was thinkin' of Kanga."

Knowing the boy's feelings for the old man, Mrs. Jones said, "Oh, I shouldn't worry. He's used to all kinds of weather."

Then she decided to see the boss later about getting a coat for the boy, though the difficulty, she thought, would be in finding one to fit him.

Alici and Maheena pattered in and out of the inside doorway that led both to the boss's quarters and the men's. Each time the girls came in with a tray or for something, they talked about the rain plopping on the roof. Their eyes rounded, wide-eyed at the rain's strangeness.

"Me never see dis kind," Alici told Mrs. Jones on one trip, while the boy listened intently. "He all the same blob, blob, blob you tip from cup. He fall 'im splash, one fella plop, not all the same rain."

She stopped, unable to find the words needed really to explain, and glanced from the boy to Mrs. Jones. Maheena nodded emphatically, bobbing her head in agreement.

Mrs. Jones agreed that the rain was falling in enormous drops, and the boy added, "Yeah, you c'n feel 'em slap on your head or the back of yer hand, like Alici says. An' they're just like a bucket bein' poured over you."

When his dinner was finished, the boy said good night and went outside. Hunched against the rain still falling in its strange leaden manner, he groped through the darkness to his room.

As he lit a lantern, he thought he heard a sound. Thinking it might be Kanga, he peered into his room, but the bare, dusty room was empty. Then the gruff coughing sound came again, and he knew it was coming from outside. From just beyond the hedge, he guessed, hurrying along with his lantern held high.

As he pushed the gate open, his wet hair chilled to an icy twitch that shivered on his neck. From the blackness beyond the lantern's glow came a snarling cough that was frightening, and gradually a huge, bristling dog crept into the lamp's light.

Unnerved, the boy stared for several seconds before he

recognized Skipper, Kanga's vicious but devoted "king" dog. The animal crouched, snarling at the boy in a growling, ferocious way, yet somehow commanding; urging him, by an occasional flick of its slavering jaws, to follow into the darkness.

The boy shivered, wondering what to do. "On my own," he thought, "I don't have a chance. Kanga might be miles an' miles away or just out there on the plains. But sure as anything he's hurt, or Skipper wouldn't be here."

Bending down, he reached to pat Skipper's head, then snatched his hand back swiftly. The dog's savage jaws snapped horribly as they missed by a fraction, and for a frightened, fleeting moment the boy wanted to run.

The dog seemed viciously overbearing in its cruel, powerful forcefulness. Yet the boy knew devotion had brought the dog to him. He could see it in the eyes, glowing through the wet, shaggy hair on the animal's scarred head.

Spitting rain from his mouth, the boy whispered, "O.K., Skipper, I'll come. There ain't time to run around lookin' for anyone else. An' I reckon if I did, you'd bolt an' leave us to it. Or tear a strip from the boss or Ross if they didn't understand yer."

Gingerly, he started to walk, now sodden right through to his skin. Skipper trotted ahead, oblivious of rain or darkness, intent only on the instincts that were leading him back to Kanga.

Gradually, the dog increased its pace, and the boy had to half run, half trot to keep up. His feet slid on the dust that had now turned to a paste, and several times he went down to his knees.

Each time his main concern was the lantern, in case it

should break or go out. But miraculously, he kept the light aloft and burning. And every panting, slippery yard he wished he was really fit; that his legs could have really run as they had when he stopped the buggy.

Gasping and sliding, with the great blobs of rain still making their weird drumming all around him, he followed Skipper into a gully. From there, the "king" dog led on until the ground underfoot started to rise as the boy toiled behind blindly. He felt numbed, almost stunned by the continuous heavy raindrops beating on his head and shoulders.

"It's as if they were little hammers," he thought, "tappin' an' tappin' an' tappin'. Beatin' on yer skin like ole Ted did that weld until you're one big blob, bruised in together."

He was struggling to the slope's crest, several feet from Skipper's eager haunches, when the darkness began to lighten. Glancing around hazily through the wetness streaming over his eyes, the boy saw a car's headlights. Lurching, bumping, and swaying, a car was coming slithering on the pasty surface of the slippery ground.

Knowing the car could only be the boss's, the boy gasped a sigh of relief.

"At least," he told Skipper when the dog peered back savagely, "I didn't have to go lookin' for 'im. He's here, lookin' for us. Now the thing is, can you go on leadin' with a car bouncin' around behind yer? Maybe it'll be best if I keep on walkin' an' they follow *me* in the car."

He said "they," certain that Ross and some men would be with the boss, ready to help if the car stuck or their help was otherwise needed.

Skipper snarled and bristled, prowling around the boy
when the car lurched close. As the boss stepped out, followed by Ross and two men, the dog crouched, ready to
spring. And a sudden wild elation flooded through the
boy. He felt the guardianship emanating from the dog. Its
stained, yellow teeth glistened warningly from its back-
drawn lips. There was no mistaking the savagery with
which it stood between him and the boss.

"He's got an idea," the boy suddenly shouted, scuffing
rain from his lips, "that yer might be goin' to stop me. I
wouldn't come too near if you don't mind me sayin'."

The boss shouted, "I won't, don't worry. But what's it
all about? I saw your lantern when I was out for a look at
the weather."

His shirt and trousers were already streaming as he stood
outlined by the headlights and flanked by Ross and the
men.

In quick, shouted sentences, the boy explained about
Skipper's arrival and his own subsequent decision to
follow the dog back in search of Kanga. This made the
boss turn to say something to Ross.

Huddled in the big, splashing drops of rain, they talked
for two or three minutes before the boss turned again to
shout, "It looks like what you say about Kanga being hurt.
But the point is, he might be miles away. An' in this"—he
jerked a hand skyward—"we've got Buckley's chance of
findin' him. How's the dog traveling? Does he seem to be
headin' straight?"

The boy thought for a moment, assessing the way he
had come. Then he shouted, "Yeah, I think so. An' if

there's nothing better, I could go on with 'im. Maybe you could follow, sort of givin' me some light."

He toned his voice to conform with making a suggestion. There was a worry in his mind that the boss or the big overseer might think he was telling them what to do.

"Sort of growin' big-headed," he mumbled as an afterthought, though only the dog could hear.

Had the boy known, both the boss and Ross were thinking the exact opposite. Hunched together again while the rain slid down their necks, they talked quickly. Ross said he couldn't see any other way than the boy had suggested, though he'd sooner do the walking and let the boy ride in the car.

"Yet," he shrugged to say, "if I did, the dog might clear out. He knows the boy as a sort of second best to Kanga."

The boss said, "Sort of second best is right. That youngster ought t' be still in bed after the bumpin' he took the other day. O.K. then, we can't stand all night talking."

Shouting to the boy to, "Go ahead, we'll follow," the boss climbed into his car, followed by the others.

Alone in the headlights, the boy turned and, motioning to Skipper, said, "All right, Skip, you c'n lead us again. We might make better time now we've got the lights behind us."

As if freed, Skipper wheeled from his snarling stance to trot on. The boy followed, still carrying the lighted lantern.

"I could blow it out," he told the wet, shaggy form in front of him. "But yer never know. The car might dip or skid some place, an' where would we be? Slap into a wall of solid darkness."

Skipper's tail held steady without sign of any recogni-
tion. One voice only could break the dog's iron shell of indifference or ease the snarl from its grim, savage jaws.

"He's like Kanga," the boy thought, struggling behind.
"Though that last time ole Kanga nearly grinned. But
Skipper, he'll never know now one inch of softness. Every
bit of feeling has been drained from him."

This thought made the boy's mind turn to another as he
slid while hurrying across a shallow depression.

"There again," he said out loud, wiping mud from his
trousers, "it's the country. Look at it now. Dust this
mornin', an' now you can't keep yer feet. An' you wouldn't
believe rain could clout you silly."

The words made him chuckle, and holding up his face
to let the rain smack into it, he added, "I'm mad. Mad as a
snake. But it don't matter. All I hope is ole Kanga ain't
too badly hurt."

In the car behind, the boss stared out under the raised
windshield. Its angle saved the rain from beating in, but
the incoming air felt damp. He could smell the steam, too,
from his own and the other men's wet clothing. And like
the boy, he was thinking about the country and the
weather; the slow, heavy splashing rain that was falling.

"If it lasts," he said thoughtfully, turning for a moment
to Ross, sitting beside him, "we're right. Another two days
of it, I reckon, an' we c'n say there's a chance. Enough to
give us a steady growth." He meant grass, which would
sprout and die unless sufficient rain fell to soak deep into
the ground.

His hand tapped the wheel as he peered ahead again to
the wet, muddy boy and big, shaggy dog. Outlined in the

beams of the skidding, lurching car's headlights, the two seemed immeasurably lonely—as if they were in a world of channeled light, hemmed in by an awful blackness.

Ross said, "Yeah, an' I think it will. Last, I mean. If I miss my guess, we're in for a real soaker. Floods almost, I'd reckon."

His eyes, fixed habitually to a gaze that searched the skylines, saw beyond boy and dog to the limits of the head-lights.

And suddenly he jerked forward to add, "So help me, there's something there. You see it? There! By that old myall tree."

Restlessly impatient with the car's crawling, slithery progress, he unlatched a door, ready to jump out.

But the boss shouted, "Hold on. You won't gain any-thing by runnin' on this," and fought with the car as it slewed around sideways.

Hunched over the wheel, he tried to see at the same time toward where Ross had pointed. The two men on the back seat both shouted that they could see something.

And ahead, Skipper leaped away from the boy. Wor-ried lest the dog should disappear from sight, the boy shouted for it to wait, then began to run faster himself. He could see a horse, droop-headed and saddled, standing near a tree. Beyond it, as he gasped through the rain, he saw Kanga's dog pack bunched on the ground.

The dogs were milling, made restless by the glare of the headlights; yet they neither barked nor raced toward the car. And the boy knew why as he ran past them. Kanga's voice still had them under control.

The giant old man was sprawled on the ground not far

from the pack. His head turned slowly as the boy approached, and half raising his sodden body, the old dogman said, "So yer made it. I reckoned the dawg 'd get to yer somehow."

He lay back and faced up to the sky again as he added, "Me leg's busted. Snapped so she's swingin'."

There was a harsh, taut finality in his voice that went beyond the boy's comprehension. He couldn't grasp the end in the old man's resignation.

Kneeling down, the boy said, "Cor, Kanga, you're wet. Sodden right through to the ground. Yer must be shiverin', lyin' there like that."

He went to button Kanga's shirt over his wide, hairy chest, but Skipper snarled, edging close to the boy. For a moment the dog stood poised, ready to bite.

Then Kanga knocked the dog sideways with his hand and said, "Sit down, dawg. You've done yer job. There's a thing or two now you'll have to learn without me havin' to tell yer."

Skipper licked the hand that had struck him, then crept to one side, where he crouched down silently watching the car arrive.

To the boy, there was heartbreaking sadness in the dog's rain-filled eyes. In Kanga, too, lying broken on the ground. His giant old body seemed longer than the boy had thought, now that it was stretched full length.

"Like that ole tree I'm always thinkin' he's like," the boy thought as Ross and the boss came to kneel beside him. "Now he's down, you sort of ache an' wish he could stand again. He don't seem right, lyin' useless."

The boss asked, "How is it, Kanga? How did it happen?"

His fingers began lightly running over the old dogman's saturated clothing. Any blood there might have been was already washed away.

Kanga said, "There ain't no need t' talk. Just help me up, an' one of yer bring me horse. I drug m'self a fair way, but the leg started twistin'." His shoulders jerked with effort, and he forced himself up to a sitting position.

Skipper growled, menacingly watchful, and the old dogman added, "Sit down, or I'll tear the hide off you."

Yet there was a great, longing movement in Kanga's arms and hands as he tried to stand—as if he wanted to reach the dog and go on with it, in the old, accustomed ways.

Ross said, "Take it easy, Kanga. Let the boss see yer leg 'n decide what to do. You've had it rough, soakin' here."

For long, waiting moments, while the only sound was the heavy beat of rain, Kanga sat motionless. The puddled water where he had lain looked deathly chill, so the boy channeled it away with his hands.

"There yer are, Kanga," he whispered. "It's better now. Yer won't get so cold from it lyin' round you."

He wished, as he scraped some wet mud from the old dogman, that there was a great pile of big warm blankets to put around him.

But Kanga sat, letting the rain run down his already sodden body, while the boss examined his leg. The two men went away, with an ax from the car, to cut scrub for splints. When they came back, they were carrying armfuls.

Without much talk, the boss worked competently, first

setting Kanga's leg straight, then strapping it to two of the scrub splints that he selected for straightness. For bandage he used his own and Ross's shirts torn into strips.

"A drop of rain," he told Ross, as they both glistened barechested in the headlights, "won't hurt us. The thing is to get him home as quick as we can. He's chilled right through, an' I don't wonder."

With a final pat, he tied the last strip of shirt into place and told the two men to help him get Kanga to the car.

As the three, with Ross also helping, went to lift Kanga, he pushed them away.

Above Skipper's savage snarling, he said, "When I'm dead, you c'n do that," and rolling over, forced himself to stand upright by using his hands and one good leg.

"All right," he added. "Give me a couple of them sticks an' I'll make it. But see to that nag of mine an' the dawgs first."

Towering, in a swaying manner that reminded the boy again of a tree, Kanga snatched the two sticks that the boss passed to him. Telling Skipper to be silent, he stood swaying, watching while his horse was stripped of saddle, bridle, and pack, then turned loose.

Beginning to lurch stiffly toward the car, he called Skipper to him and said, "You'll be on yer own, so watch what you're doin'. One foot wrong, an' you're for it."

Then, the watching men and boy saw something that was almost unbelievable. The old dogman stopped and just for a moment touched the "king" dog's head. Its shaggy wetness trembled, unused to the kindness.

"So there you are," the boy thought, following Kanga

on to the car. "Somewhere in him there's a bit like the rest of us. You could call it softness, but it's love. He loves that dawg more 'n anything. Even his own life, I reckon."

And as we watched Kanga struggle into the car unaided, the boy asked, "Will I walk home with 'em, Kanga? It might sort of help if they know someone's with 'em."

He gestured around at the dogs, creeping closer to the car and keening softly at Kanga's strange behavior. The boy and silent men could see that the dogs' eyes, bright in the headlights' glare, were begging—asking, almost, that they could stay close to their master.

But Kanga said, "No. They'll follow. The pace we'll travel won't be more 'n a trot to 'em."

So the boy climbed in, to sit crushed wetly between Kanga and Bede, one of the stockmen. The other squashed in on the front seat with Ross and the boss.

When the car started, it slithered in a semicircle before gradually beginning to move forward. Behind, the dogs, herded by Skipper, followed the big bay horse, which in turn followed the car.

"You wouldn't believe it," the boy thought, trying to peer over his shoulder through the teeming darkness. "They're all out there, paddin' along patient an' quiet, because Kanga's in here. They don't ask questions. Just put their heads down an' follow. You couldn't ask more, not if you tried."

A twisting, screwing lurch spun the car sideways, and while the boss braced at the wheel, fighting to straighten the car, the boy tried to arch away from Kanga but couldn't. His whole weight seemed to crush toward the old dogman, and he felt the scrub splints press into his own legs.

"Sorry, Kanga," he whispered, and heard Kanga's groan.

It seemed unreal, coming from the grim, tight jaws that the boy knew were clenched in the darkness. So unreal that any further words choked in the boy's throat.

Then, as if deciding that preliminaries were over, the rain suddenly ceased for a moment, poising the darkness ahead into a jet-black waiting bareness, pierced by the headlights.

As suddenly as it had poised, waiting, the darkness burst again to a torrential downpour that spewed over the car in a wild, blinding sheet. How the boss managed to steer or know where he was going baffled the boy as he hunched between Kanga and Bede.

Yet, when on a final, lurching skid, the car bumped headlong into a tree and came to a stop, Ross prepared to get out as he said, "Well, here we are. Yer did a good job, boss, but I'd 've never believed you'd use one of these old peppercorns for a stopper."

The boss said, "On a night like this, a man'd use anything. So help me, there must be six inches of water underfoot."

Stepping out at the same time as Ross and the stockman, he splashed into water up to his ankles.

What followed seemed to the boy to be a hazy swirl of blinding, drenching water that numbed him through completely. Somewhere in the haze, he heard the boss telling him and Bede to look after the dogs and horse.

But Kanga forced himself out of the car much as he had forced himself in and whistled shrilly. With the dogs and horse following his reeling, staggering shape, he headed for the stables. There he saw the horse fed and the dogs shut into previously empty stalls.

Afterward, dragging the broken leg across sodden ground and through swirling water, he headed for his room in the bunkhouse.

Torn between emotions he couldn't separate, the boy followed. And behind him again came Ross and the two stockmen, head-bent against the driving, smothering downpour.

"He's mad," the boy heard Bede shout to Ross. "Mad as a snake. He'll die after this, for sure."

The words chilled the boy more than the rain. He wanted to splash after Kanga and put an arm on the old man's shoulder, hurry him quickly into warmth and shelter. But he knew the old dogman's fierceness, his iron, self-willed strength, which alone was keeping him moving.

"It's only 'im," the boy thought, "who could do it. There's something within him you wouldn't find in anyone else."

Kanga's instincts stopped him at the garden gate, and the boy brushed around him to open it. A lantern, hung streaming in the rain, outlined murkily the bunkhouse steps along the garden path.

The boss had gone ahead, straight from the car, to find Mrs. Jones. The two were in Kanga's room with a great heap of blankets as the old dogman arrived.

The boy remembered seeing Mrs. Jones's quick, anxious glance pass from Kanga to his own sodden state, then the haze seemed to deepen. He felt Ross grip his arm, then a great drowsy tiredness.

When he awoke, the darkness had changed to a gray, leaden murk. Rain was still falling, cascading down from the roof. And as the memories of the night came back to him, he drew down into the warmth of his blankets. He wanted to stay secure from the rain and the inevitability of learning about Kanga.

Then he sighed, glad to sleep again for a moment. Someone had taken his clothes to dry them. He could see his boots, tipped upside down to drain, but no shirt and trousers. Burrowing deeper into the warmth, he covered his head with the blankets.

"Later," he thought as he fell asleep, "I'll see ole Kanga. He mightn't be as bad as I think he is."

And in the next room, Kanga snored softly, deep in a heavy sleep. His last defiant flounderings had sapped even his great strength. Now he lay, drugged in a sleep that was to save him, as the rain was to save Yamboorah, once the clouds had swirled away.

This book is a continuation of the story that chronicles the life of a boy on an isolated cattle-station in Outback Australia. I first wrote of him in *Boy Alone*, where he acquired his dog, Rags; secondly, in *The Roan Colt*, where he became the owner of a saddle and of the colt he named Roany. At the end of both books, my notes explained conditions as they prevailed in the early 1930's, and still prevail today, in the vast, sparsely populated heart of Australia.

Now, in this third book, *Rain Comes to Yamboorah*, the boy is of a necessity slowly maturing to those same harsh, barren conditions, one of the most important of which is the country's need of rain.

In the portents heralding the rain's coming, subtle changes occur both in the people and in other forms of life on the great, sprawling property of Yamboorah. Snakes begin to appear in greater numbers; ibis fly in vee-shaped flights, winging against the sun; emus lay their eggs on the bare, dusty earth so that the chicks will hatch into a fresh green world after the rains. The boy is aware of all these things, though he cannot quite understand what they actually portend.

As in the previous books, many of the incidents in this story actually happened, though again not necessarily in sequence. The characters, too, are based on real people, though their names are fictional. This third book of the trilogy takes a phase of the boy's life full circle. He is able to repay old Kanga for an enduring debt—that of saving his life—and also for helping him to become the owner of Rags and Roany.

I wrote the first two books in memory of a dog and a horse respectively—two animals I shall always remember. This book is in memory of a man, who in his quiet, sure way molded much of my manner of thinking. He was a fine man, as tough and as real as old Kanga.

R.O.